HOT AIR

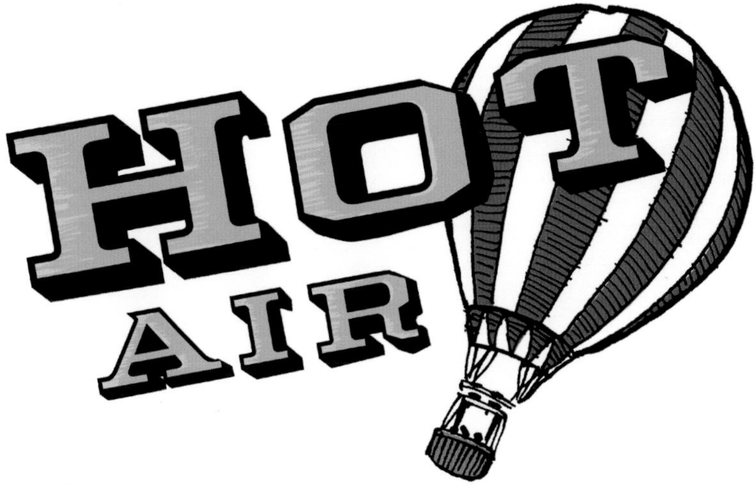

by Anthony Masters

Illustrated by Mike Perkins

Librarian Reviewer
Allyson A.W. Lyga
Library Media/Graphic Novel Consultant
Fulbright Memorial Fund Scholar, author

Reading Consultant
Elizabeth Stedem
Educator/Consultant, Colorado Springs, CO
MA in Elementary Education, University of Denver, CO

STONE ARCH BOOKS
Minneapolis San Diego

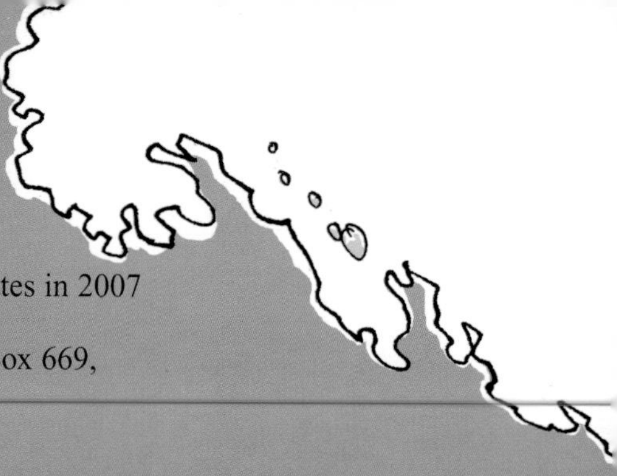

First published in the United States in 2007
by Stone Arch Books,
151 Good Counsel Drive, P.O. Box 669,
Mankato, Minnesota 56002.
www.stonearchbooks.com

Originally published in Great Britain in 2002
by A & C Black Publishers Ltd,
38 Soho Square, London, W1D 3HB.

Library of Congress Cataloging-in-Publication Data
Masters, Anthony, 1940–
Hot Air / by Anthony Masters; illustrated by Mike Perkins.
p. cm. — (Graphic Trax)
ISBN-13: 978-1-59889-086-0 (hardcover)
ISBN-10: 1-59889-086-7 (hardcover)
ISBN-13: 978-1-59889-232-1 (paperback)
ISBN-10: 1-59889-232-0 (paperback)
1. Graphic novels. I. Perkins, Mike. II. Title. III. Series.
PN6727.M246H68 2007
741.5'973—dc22 2006006069

Summary: A hot air balloon ride seems like a pretty cool birthday present for Steve, until his uncle collapses and loses control of the balloon. Then the balloon starts to drift toward the ocean.

Art Director: Heather Kindseth
Colorist: Mary Bode
Graphic Designer: Kay Fraser
Production Artist: Keegan Gilbert

1 2 3 4 5 6 11 10 09 08 07 06

Printed in the United States of America.

TABLE OF CONTENTS

Cast of Characters

STEVE

UNCLE HARRY

BUSTER

WILL

JOE

Chapter One

Steve watched Uncle Harry climb out of the basket. He was about to unhitch the balloon's mooring rope.

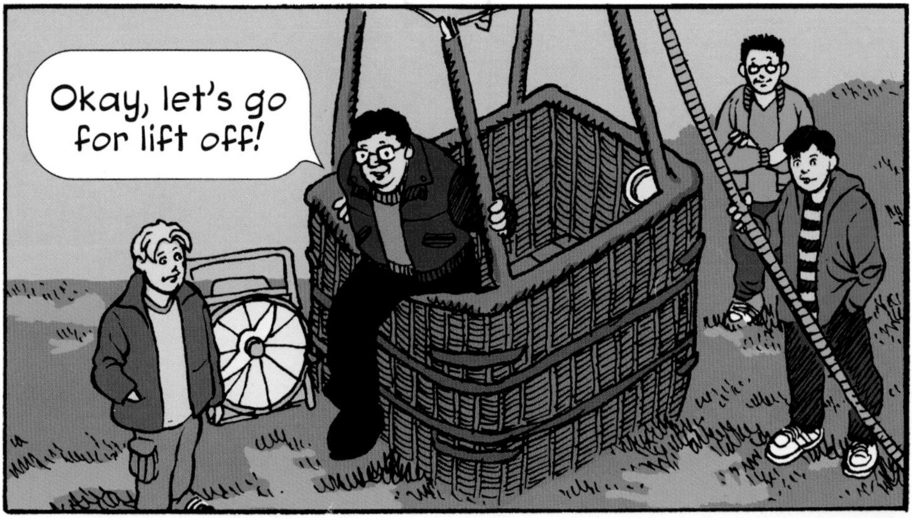
Okay, let's go for lift off!

He grinned at Steve.

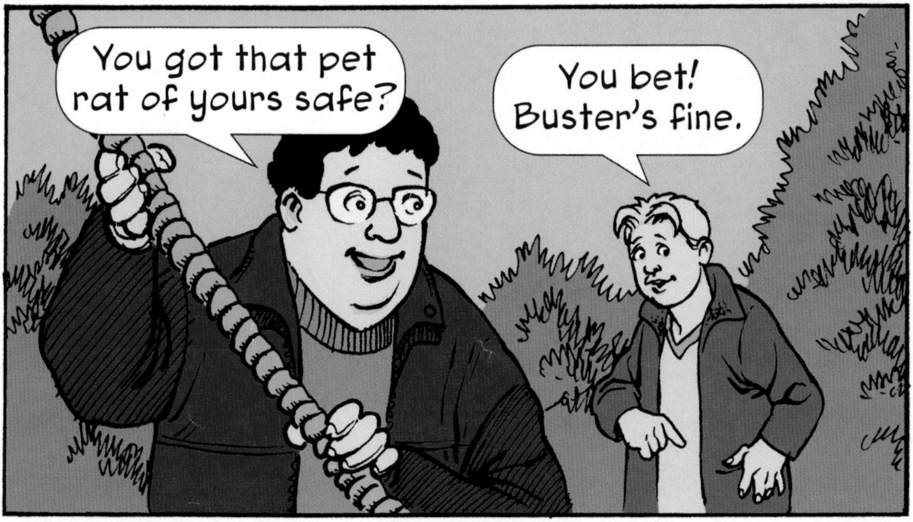
You got that pet rat of yours safe?
You bet! Buster's fine.

A muffled squeak came from Steve's pocket.

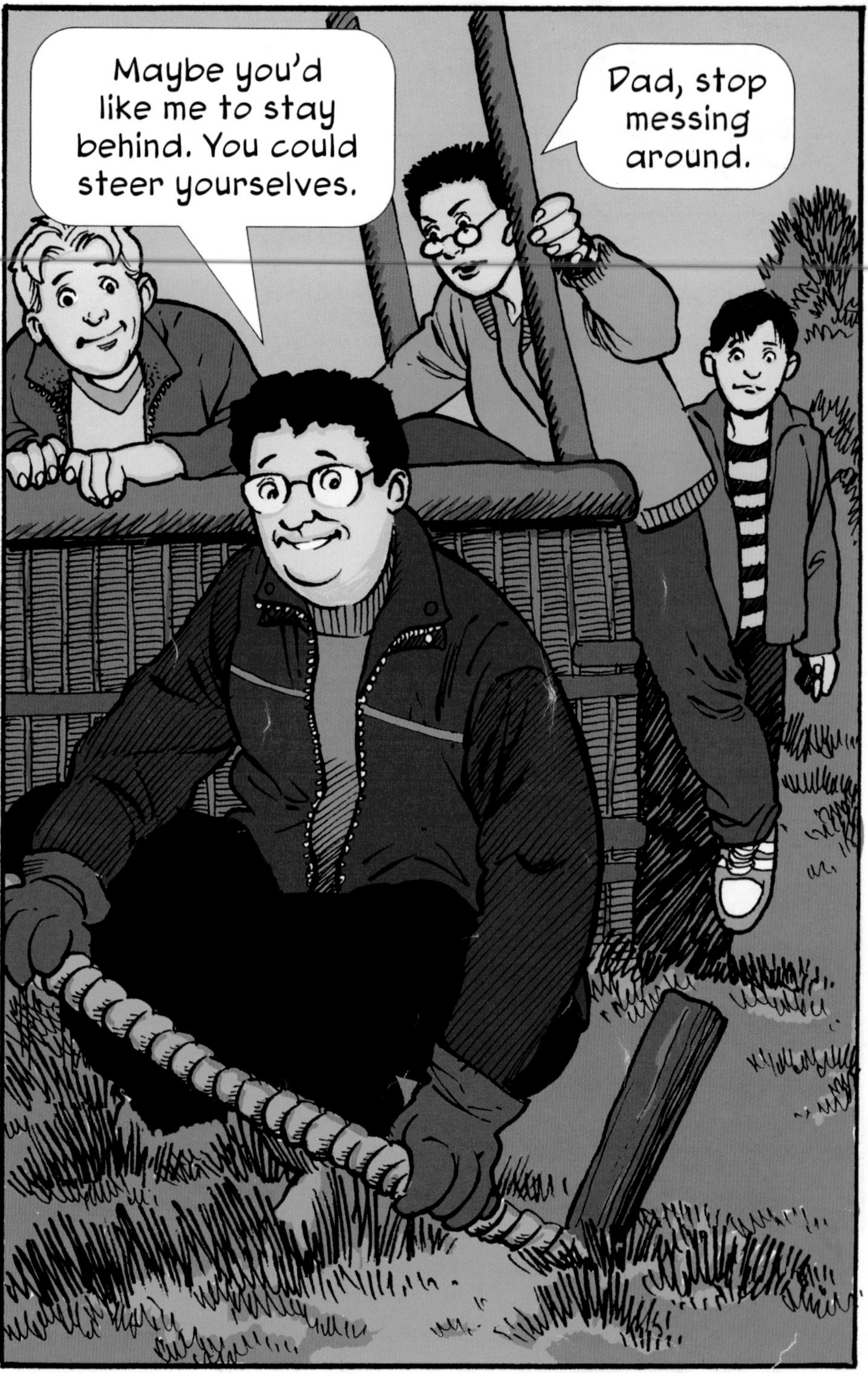
Maybe you'd like me to stay behind. You could steer yourselves.
Dad, stop messing around.

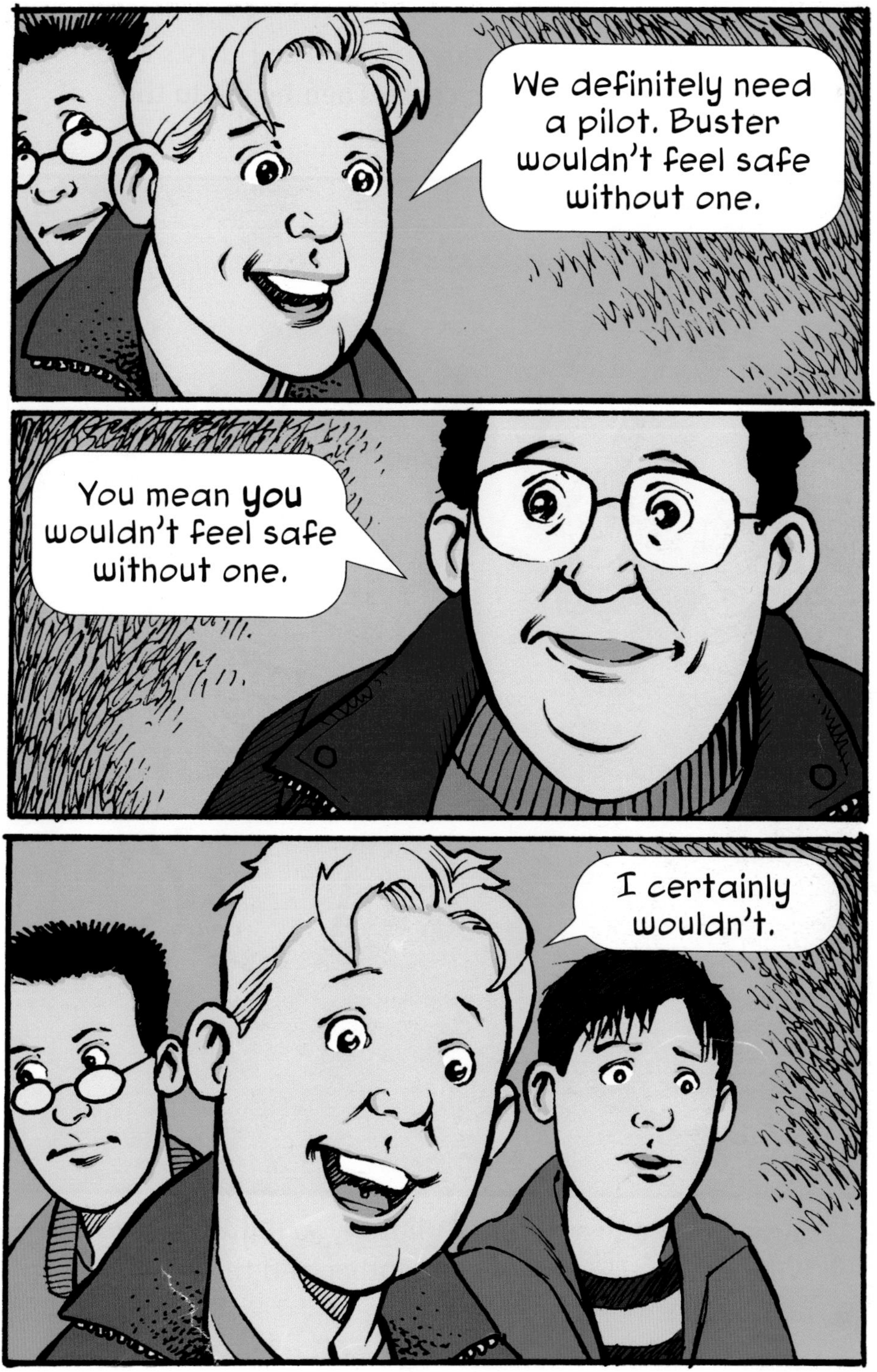
We definitely need a pilot. Buster wouldn't feel safe without one.
You mean **you** wouldn't feel safe without one.
I certainly wouldn't.

Suddenly, a funny look came over Uncle Harry's face, and his hand grabbed his chest. Then he fell to the ground, gasping for breath.

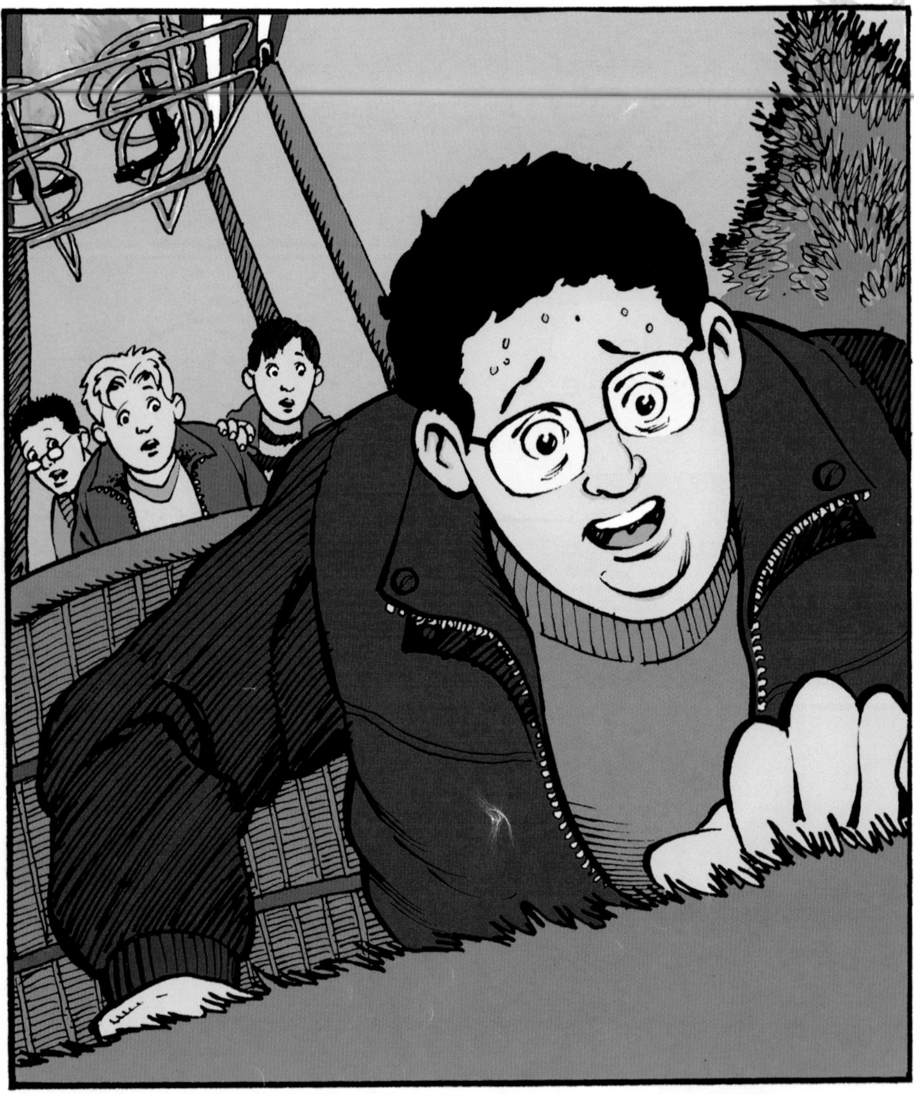

Steve gazed down at him in horror. So did his cousins, Will and Joe. Harry was their father and they could see he was sick.

Buster squeaked in alarm and Steve tickled his back to comfort him.

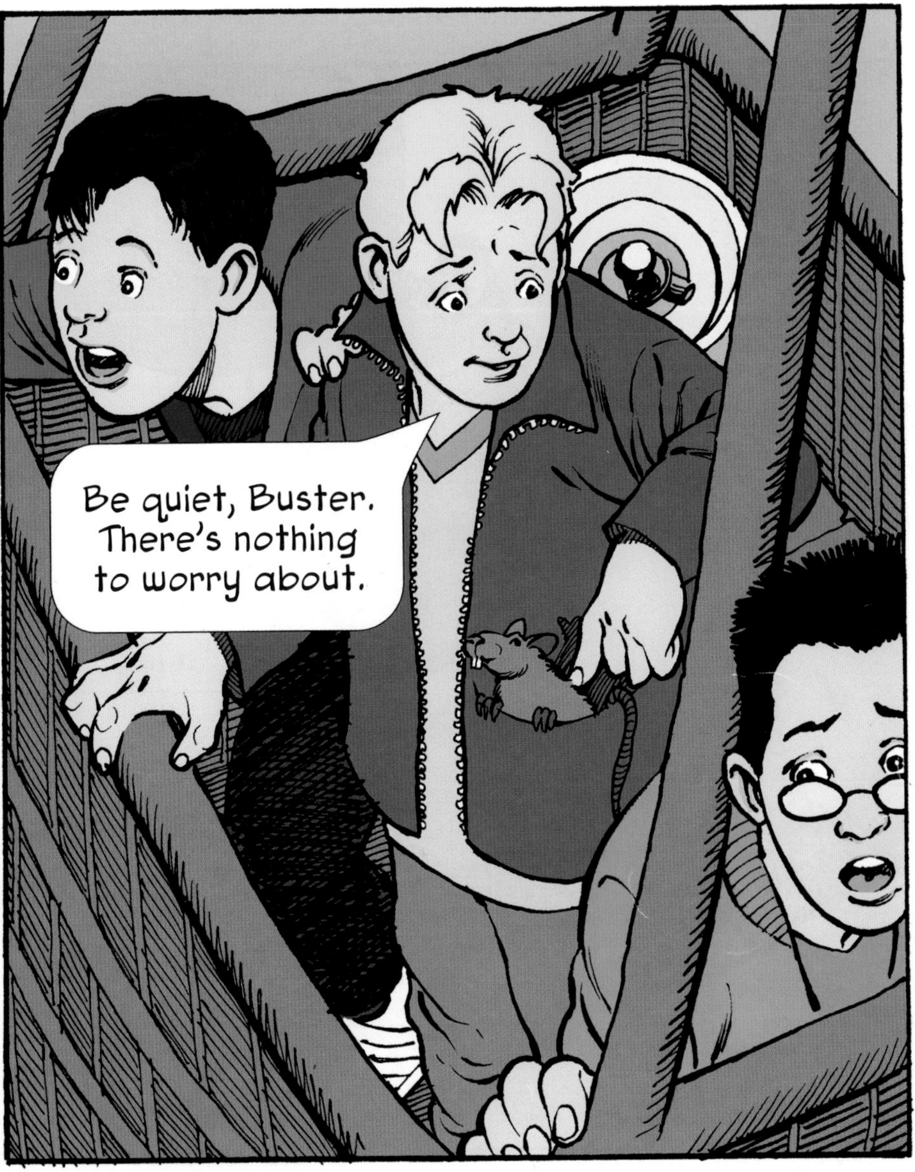
Be quiet, Buster. There's nothing to worry about.

But he was only trying to keep his cousins calm. There was everything to worry about.

Uncle Harry had dropped the mooring rope and the balloon was slowly floating up into the gray sky.

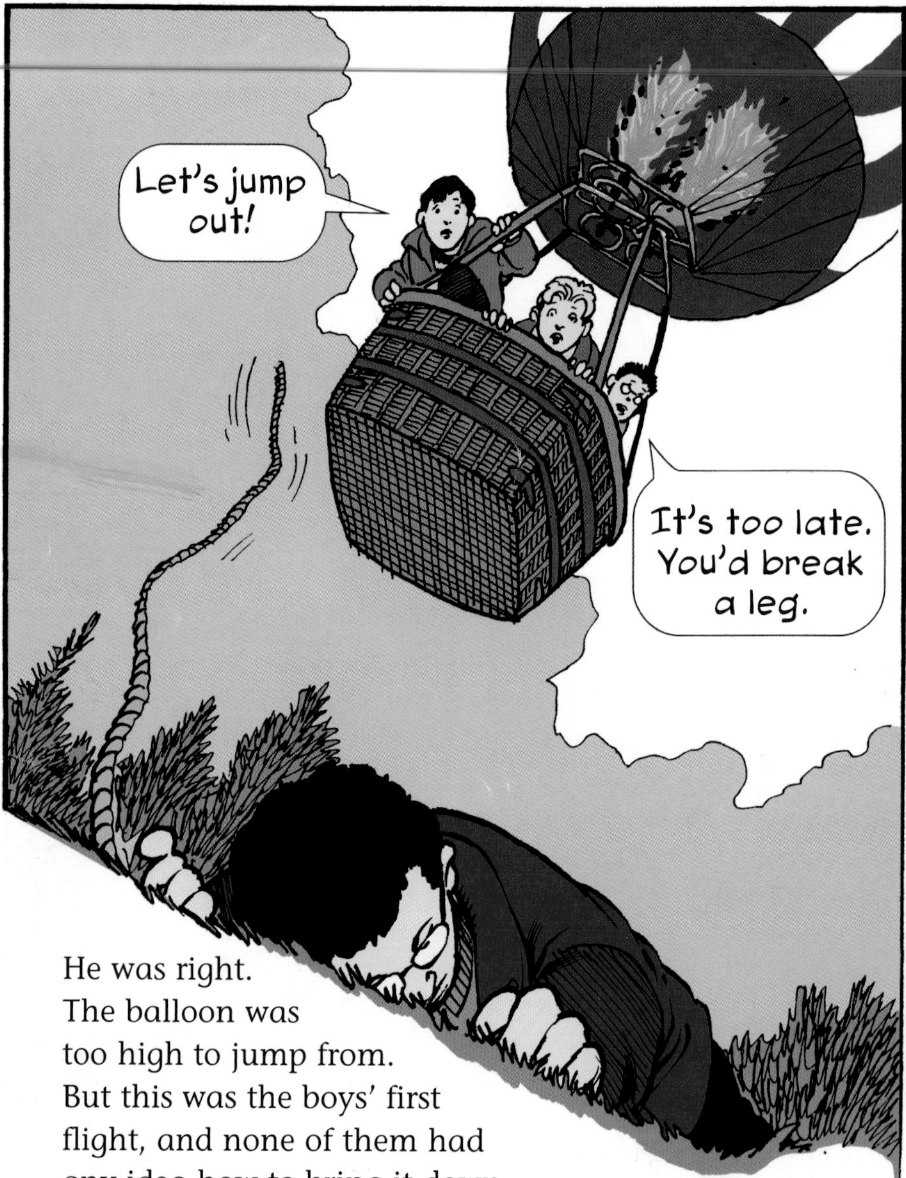
Let's jump out!
It's too late. You'd break a leg.

He was right.
The balloon was too high to jump from.
But this was the boys' first flight, and none of them had any idea how to bring it down.

The red flame of the burner roared above them.

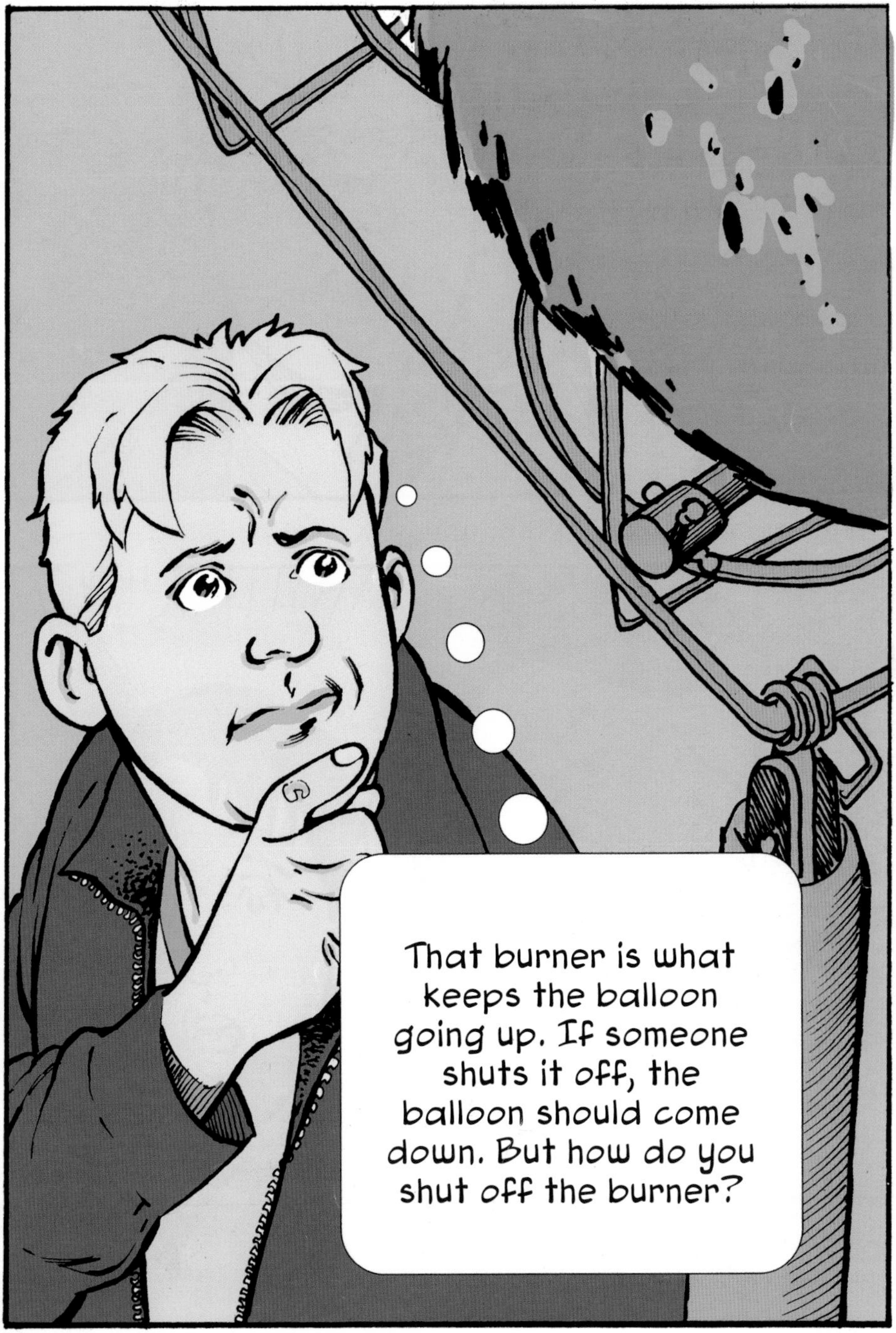
That burner is what keeps the balloon going up. If someone shuts it off, the balloon should come down. But how do you shut off the burner?

Steve's throat was so dry he could hardly speak.

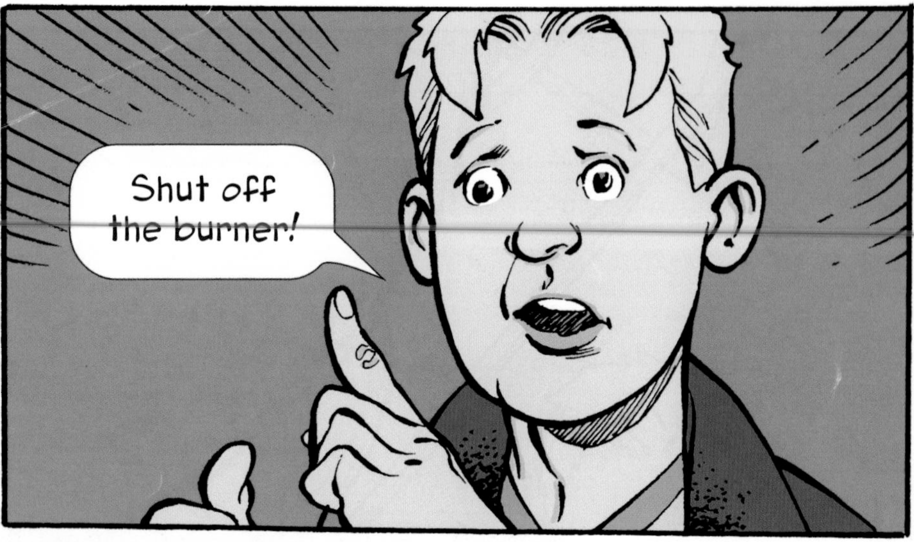
Shut off the burner!

Will and Joe looked at him uneasily.

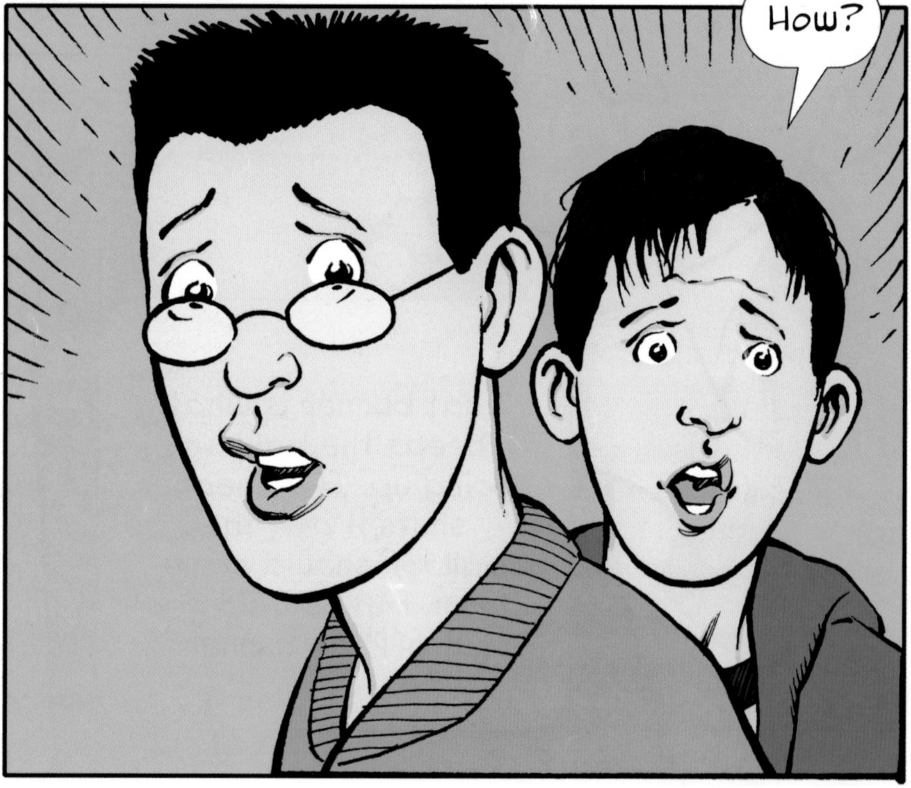
How?

Chapter Two

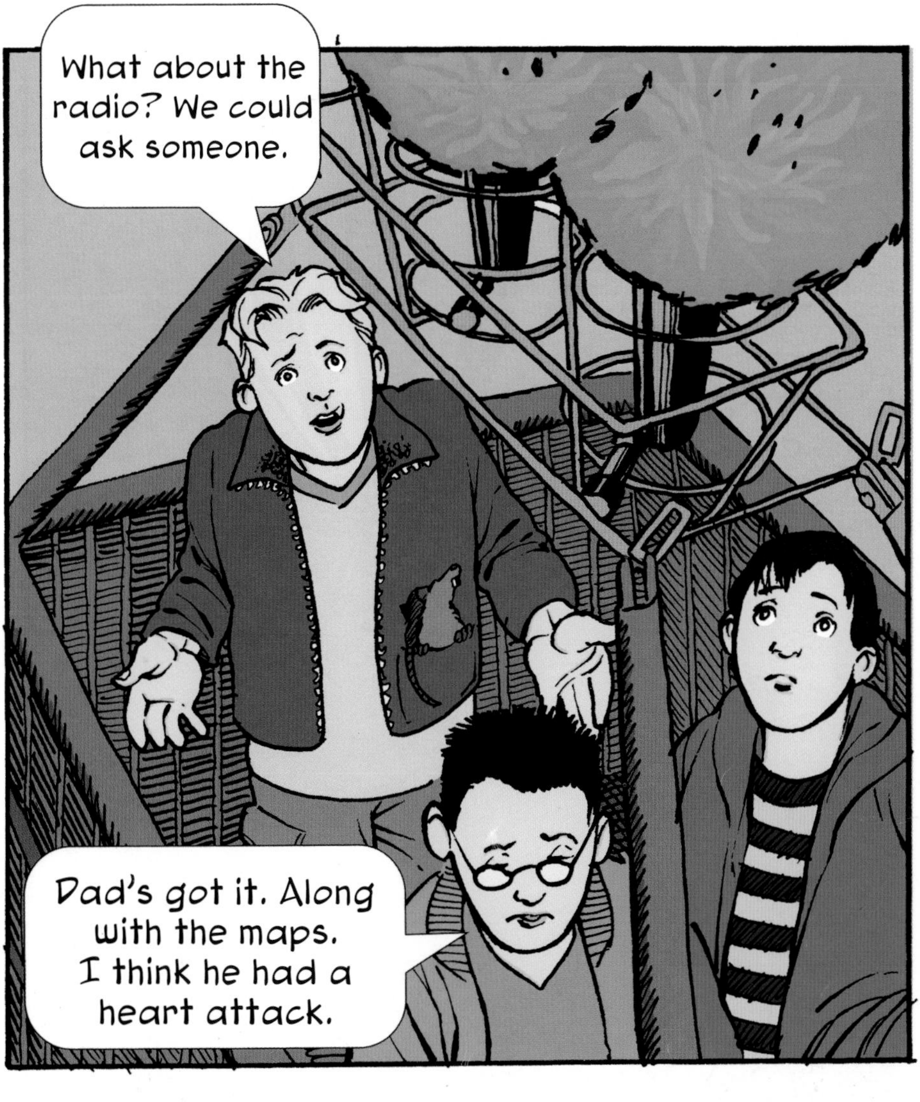
What about the radio? We could ask someone.
Dad's got it. Along with the maps. I think he had a heart attack.

Will's voice broke. None of the boys wanted to show how scared they were.

Steve looked down. He figured that they were several hundred feet above the ground already, and Uncle Harry was still lying in the field. There was no one else around.

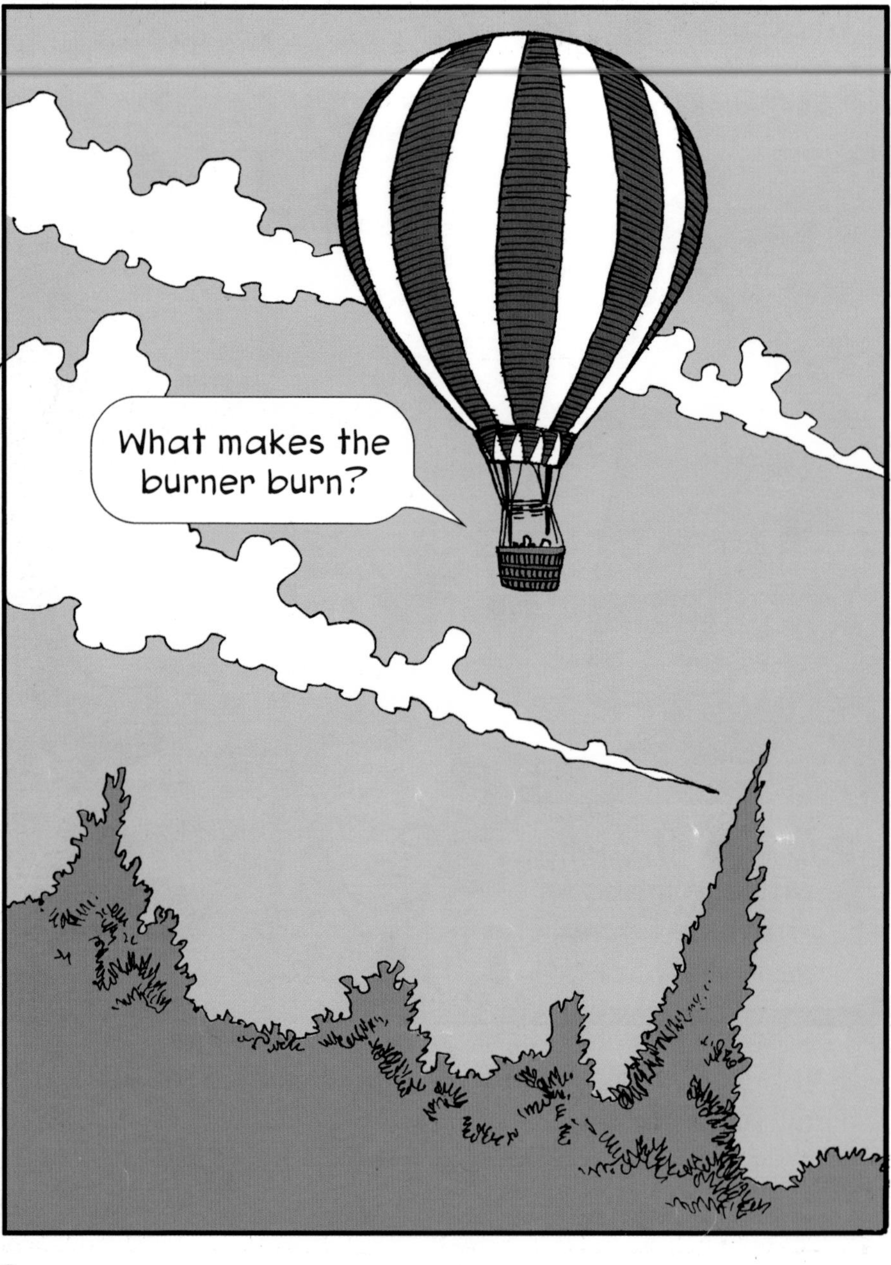
What makes the burner burn?

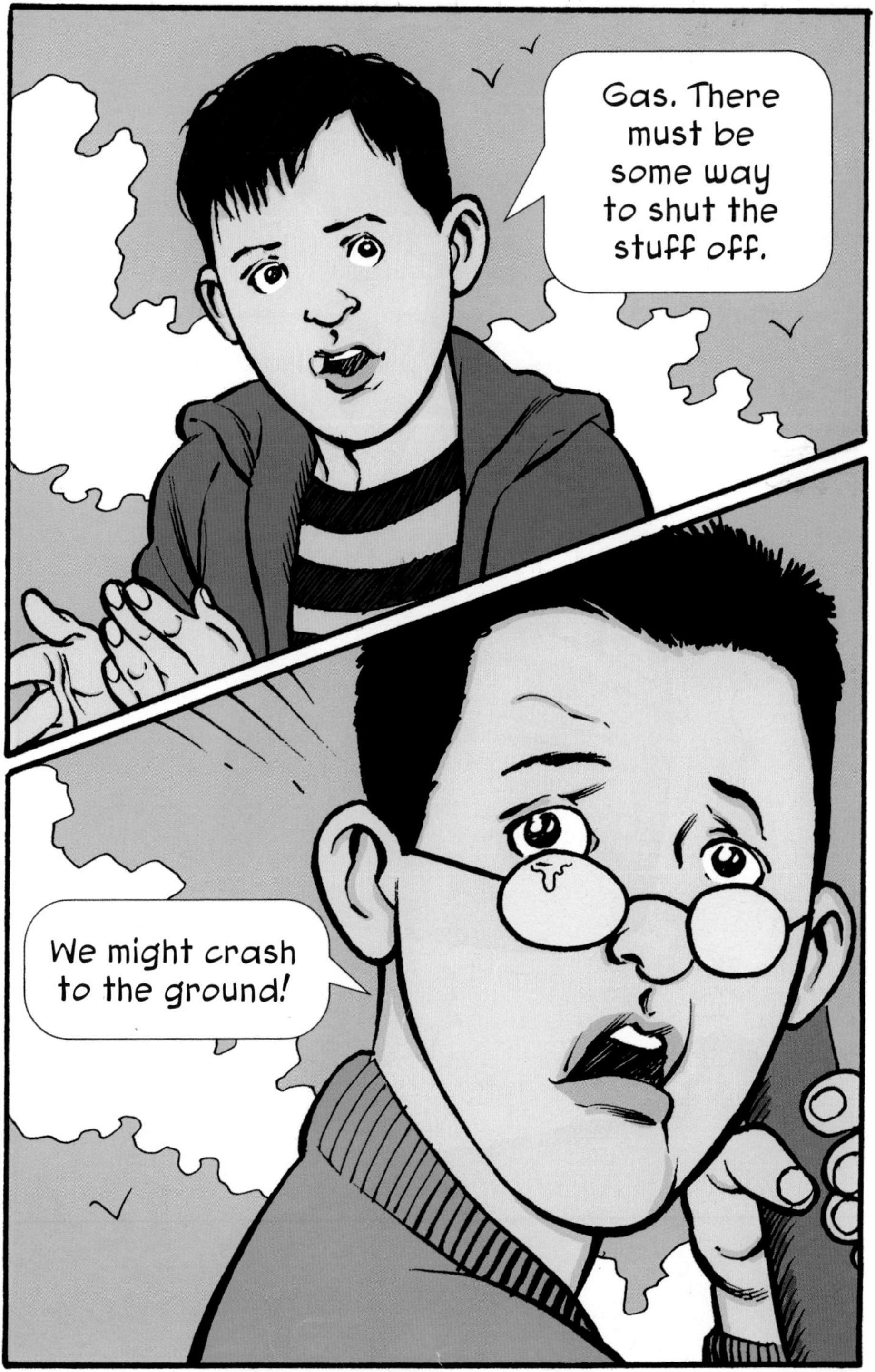
Gas. There must be some way to shut the stuff off.
We might crash to the ground!

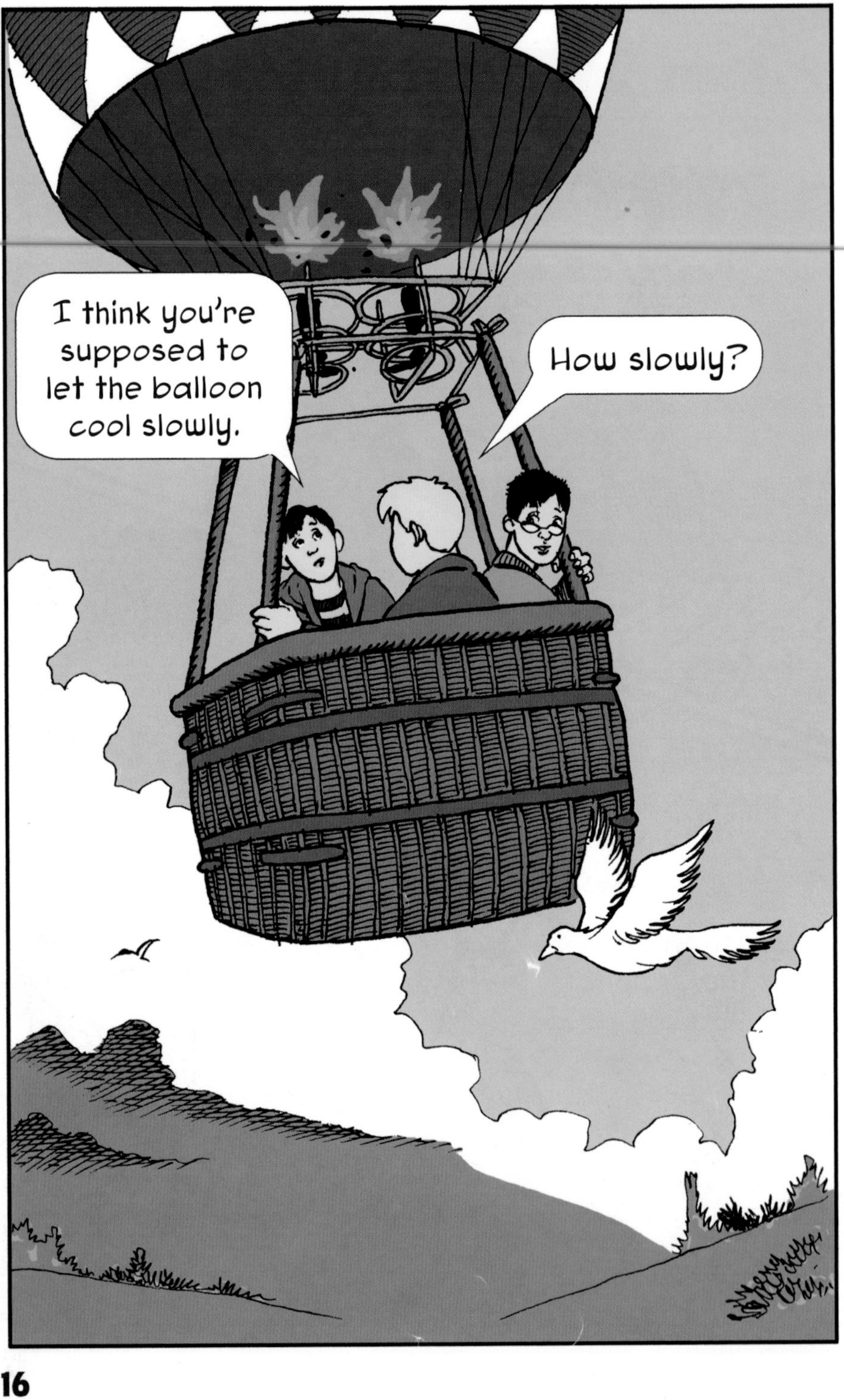
I think you're supposed to let the balloon cool slowly.
How slowly?

No one replied. Instead, Steve gazed up at the large red and white balloon. It was starting to get windy and there were dark storm clouds on the horizon.

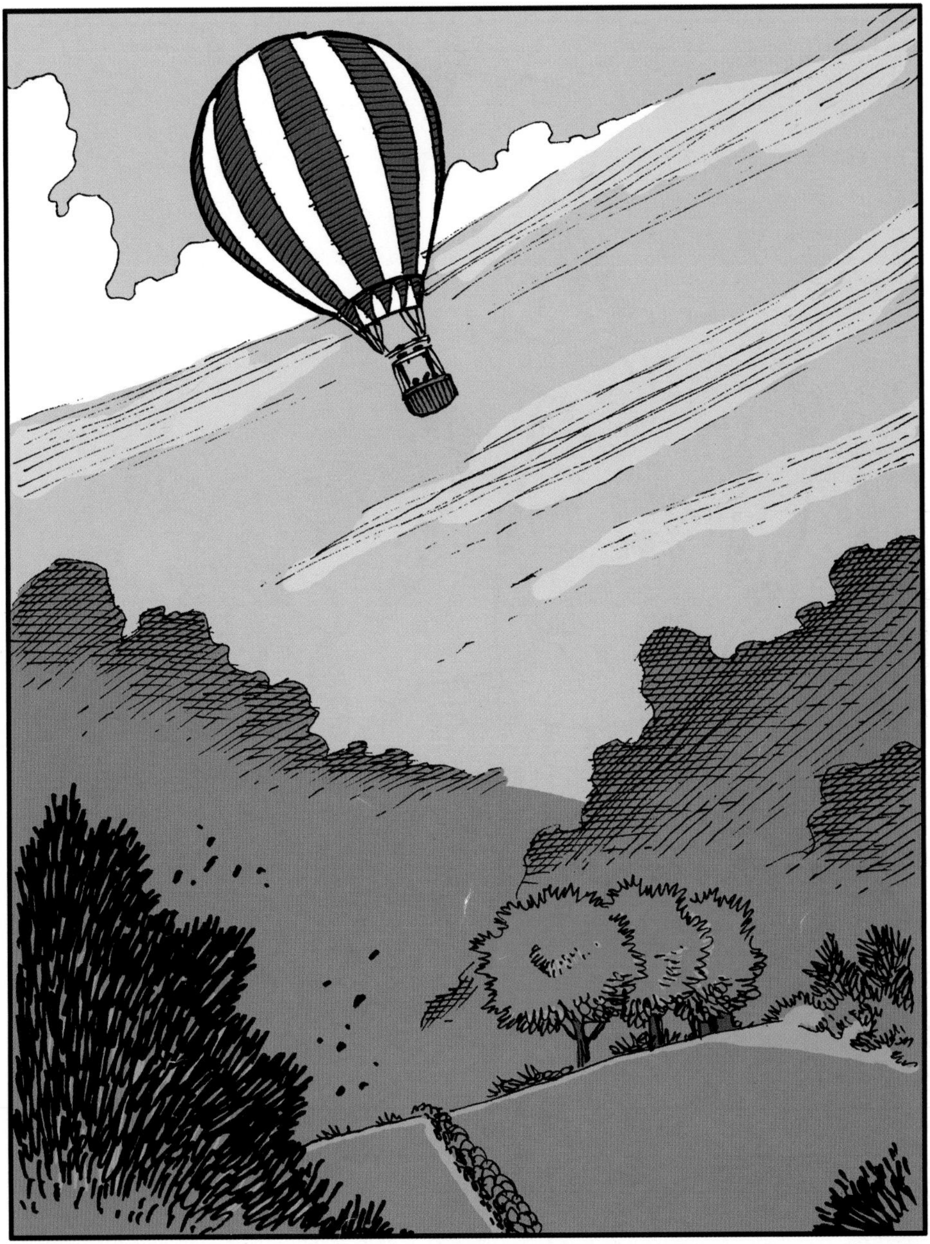

Steve had been looking forward to his first trip in a hot air balloon. Today he was eleven years old and this was his birthday treat. Some treat, he thought. The balloon was moving faster now.

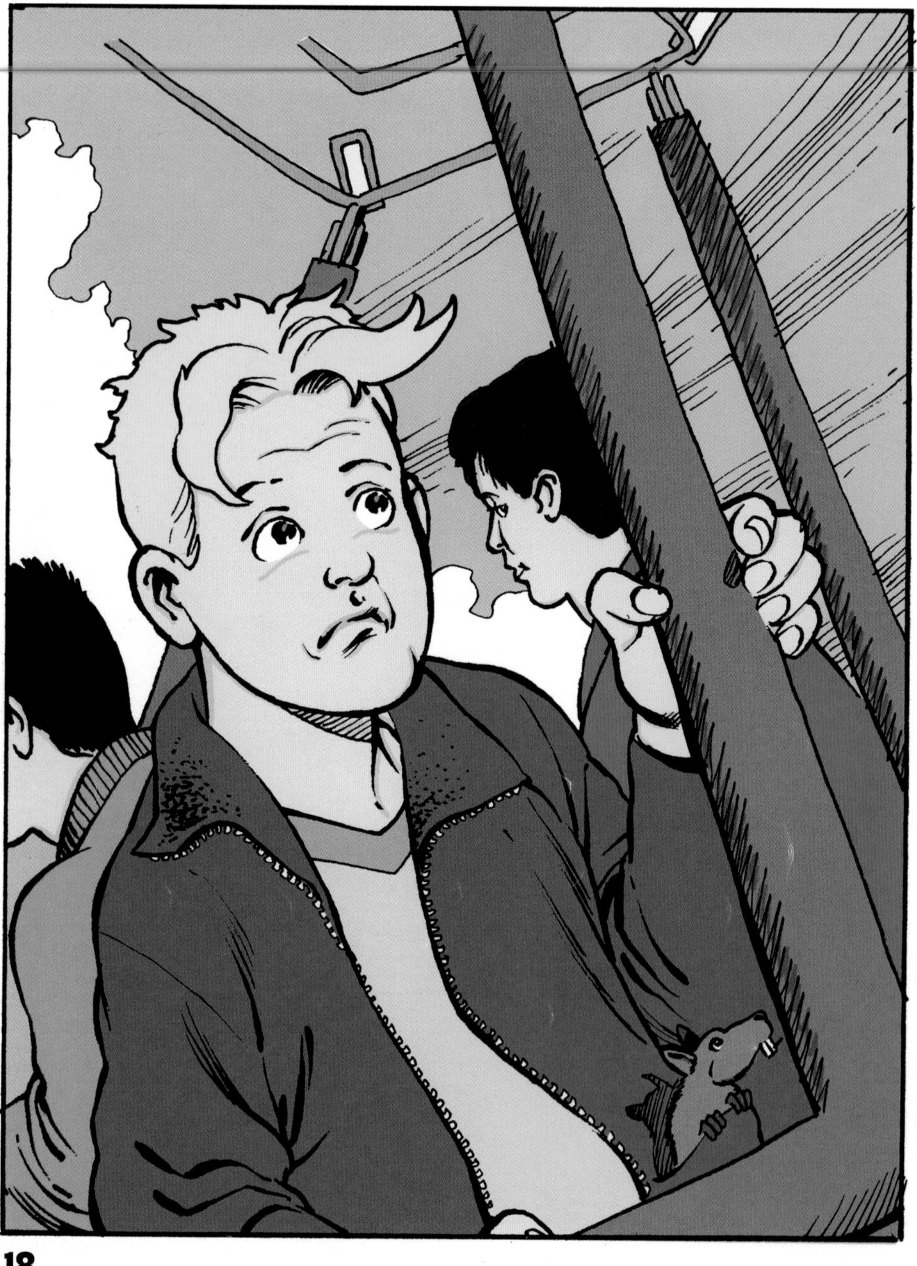

Will and Joe were twins, a year younger than Steve. They looked helpless. Somehow Steve knew he had to make the decisions. He examined the burner and saw a brass toggle.

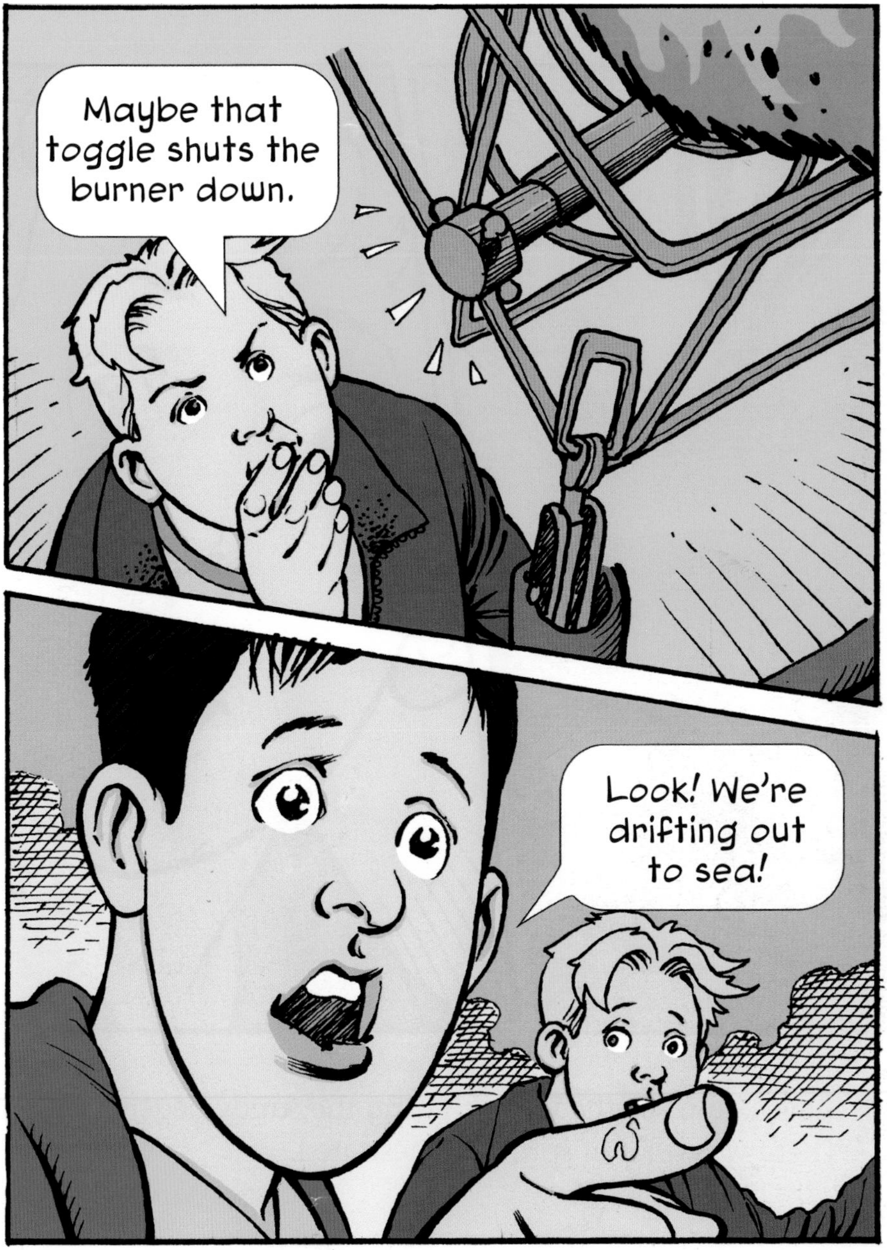
Maybe that toggle shuts the burner down.
Look! We're drifting out to sea!

Steve looked over the side of the basket. The ground was much farther away and they were heading for the cliffs. Beyond the cliffs was the sea. The wind was still rising. So was the balloon.

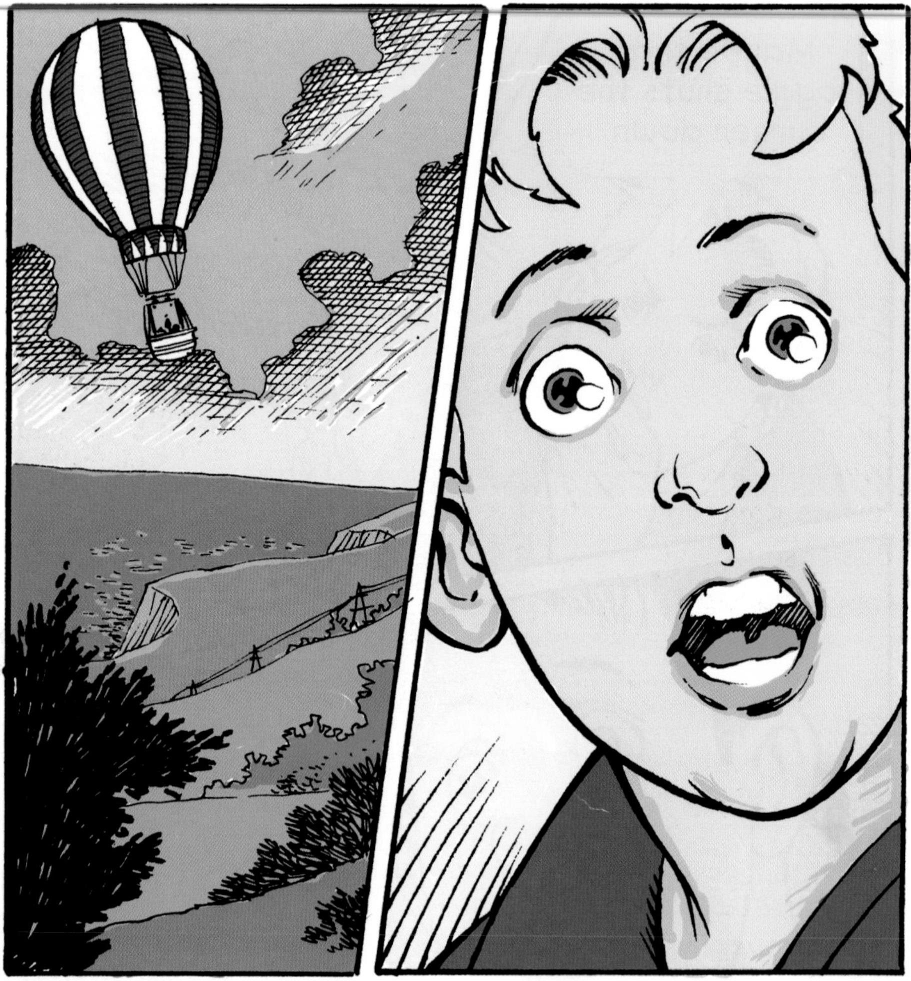

Steve could see the waves hitting the sandy beach. There was a lot of spray. He hesitated.

Then, thinking quickly, Steve pulled at the toggle and the burner shut down.

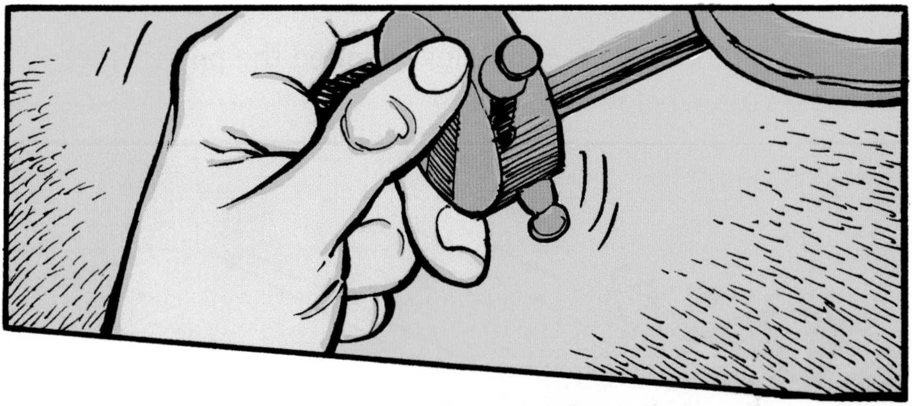

There was no more roaring. No more flames. The balloon began to drift down toward the cliffs. Buster squeaked and struggled.

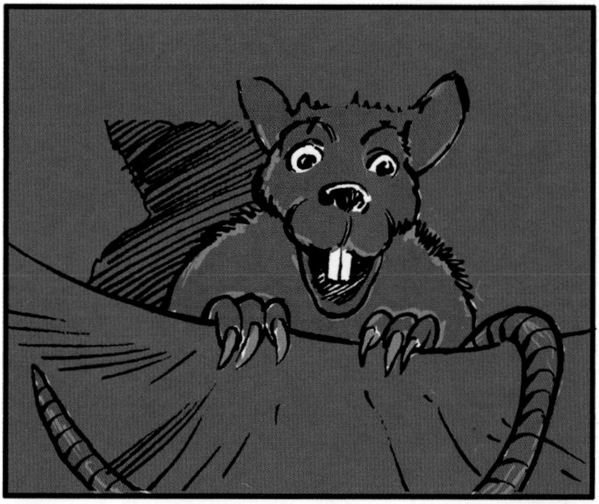

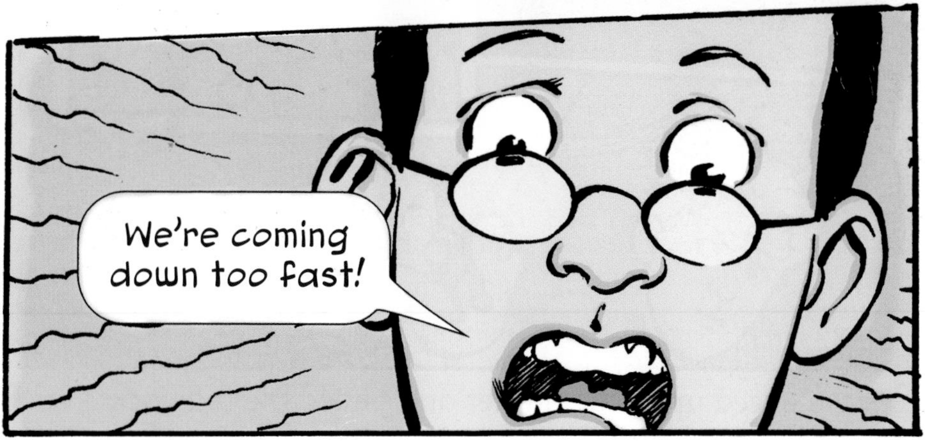
We're coming down too fast!

Chapter Three

As the balloon lost height, Steve spotted the power lines in the valley below the cliffs.

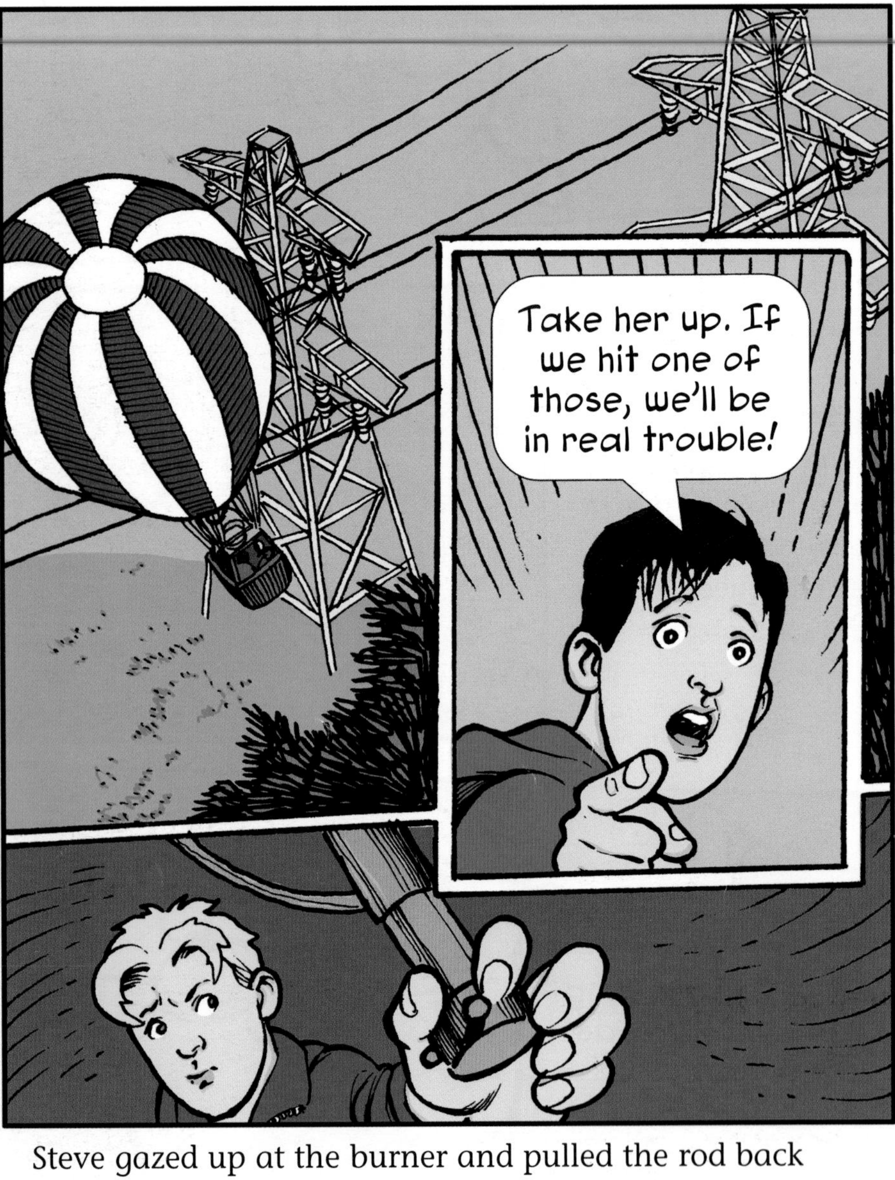
Take her up. If we hit one of those, we'll be in real trouble!

Steve gazed up at the burner and pulled the rod back into its original position.

Nothing happened and the balloon continued to drift down. Suddenly, the burner fired and the bright red flame flared. The balloon began to rise again, but Steve was sure he waited too long to clear the power lines. The towers loomed up at them like giant steel fingers.

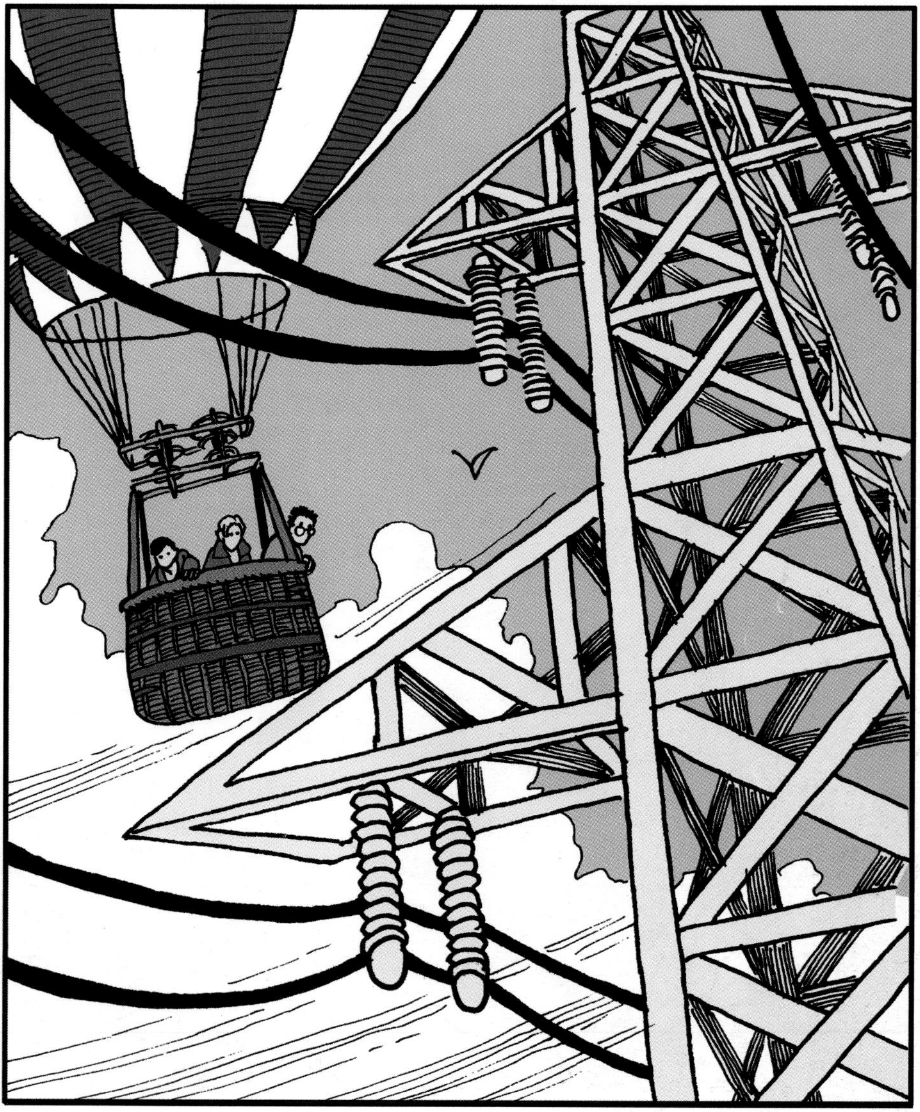

Then, just as they were bracing themselves for the collision, the balloon suddenly soared, clearing the lines by a few inches.

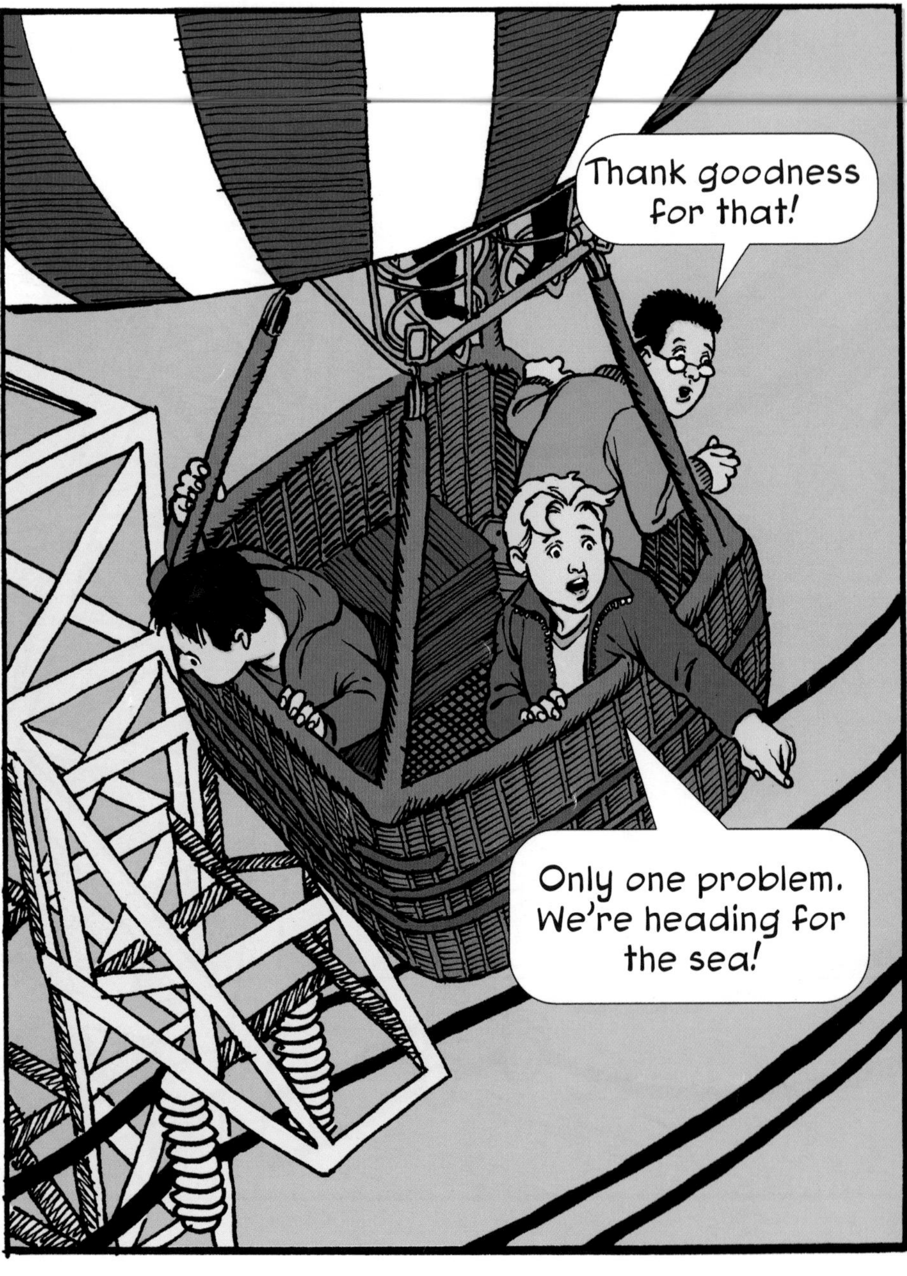
Thank goodness for that!
Only one problem. We're heading for the sea!

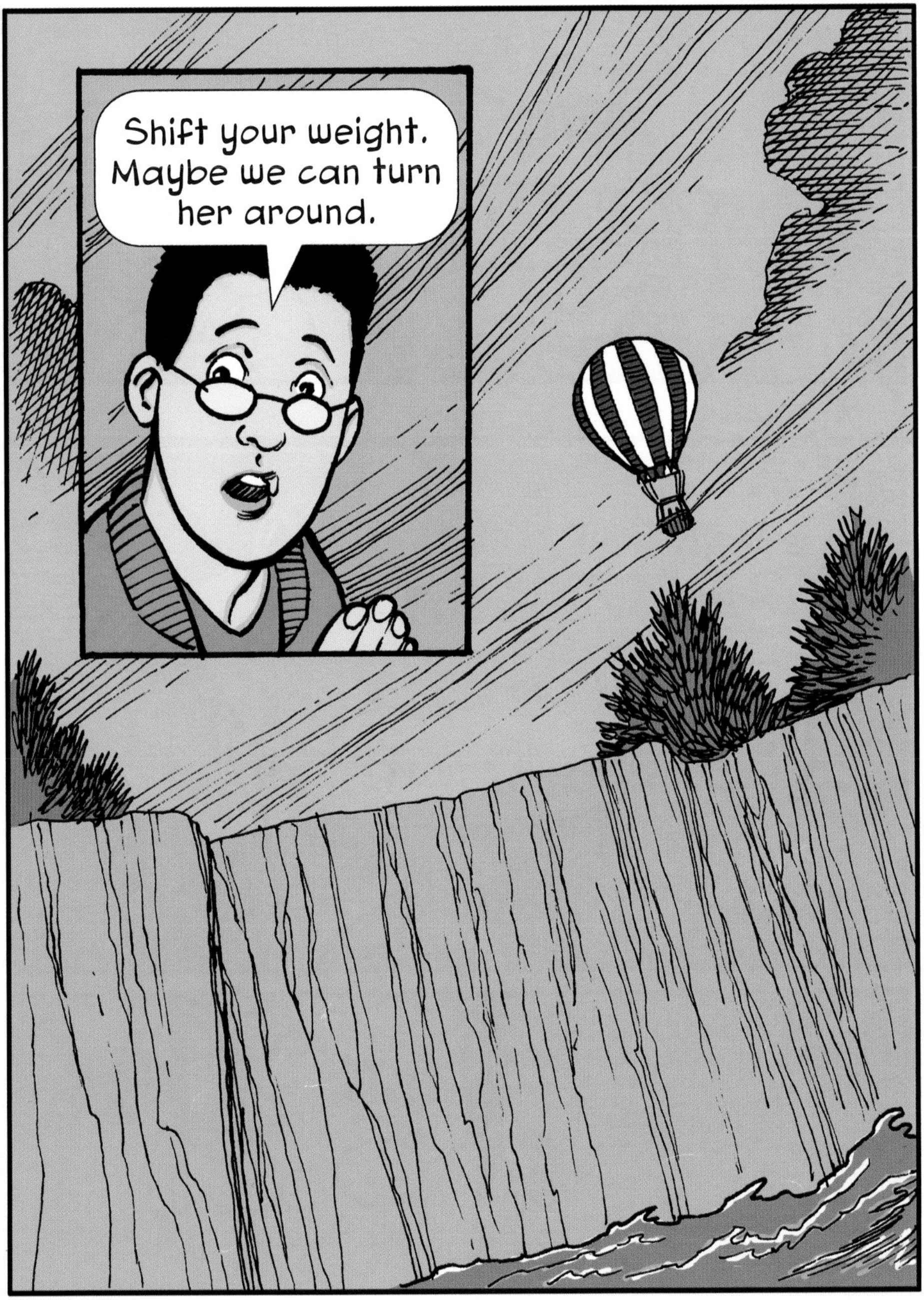
Shift your weight. Maybe we can turn her around.

The basket rocked back and forth. The wind was too strong, and they kept heading toward the sea.

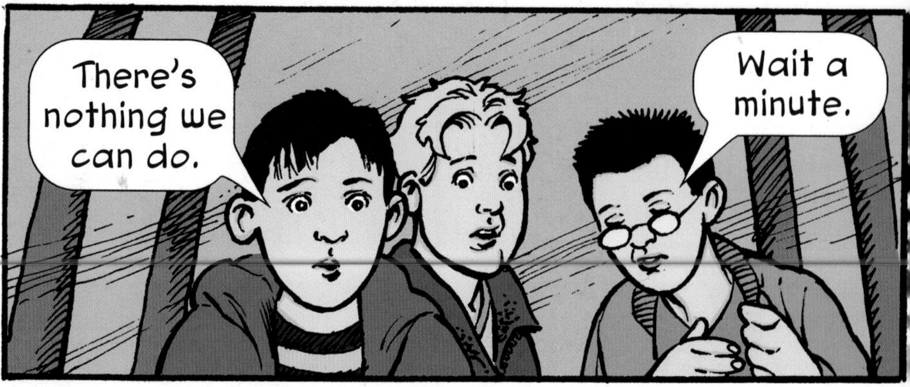
There's nothing we can do.
Wait a minute.

Will grabbed his cell phone.

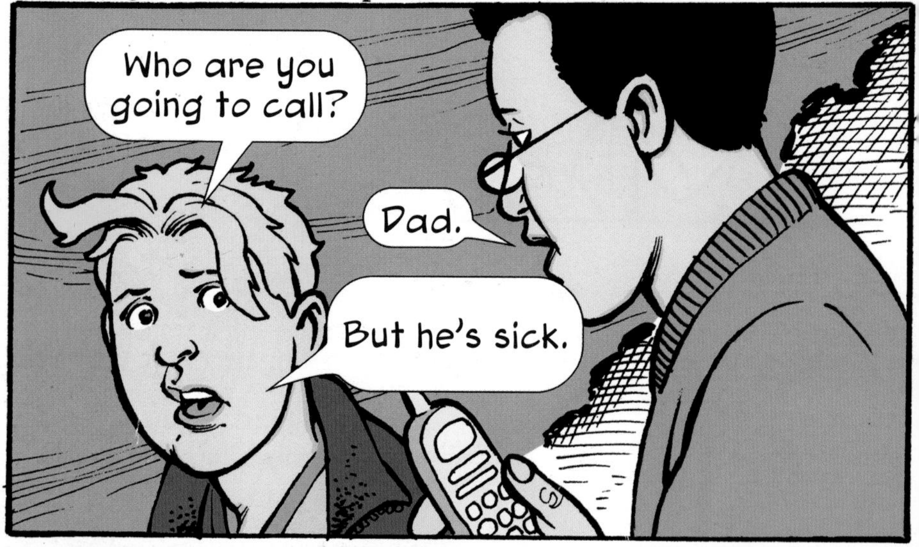
Who are you going to call?
Dad.
But he's sick.

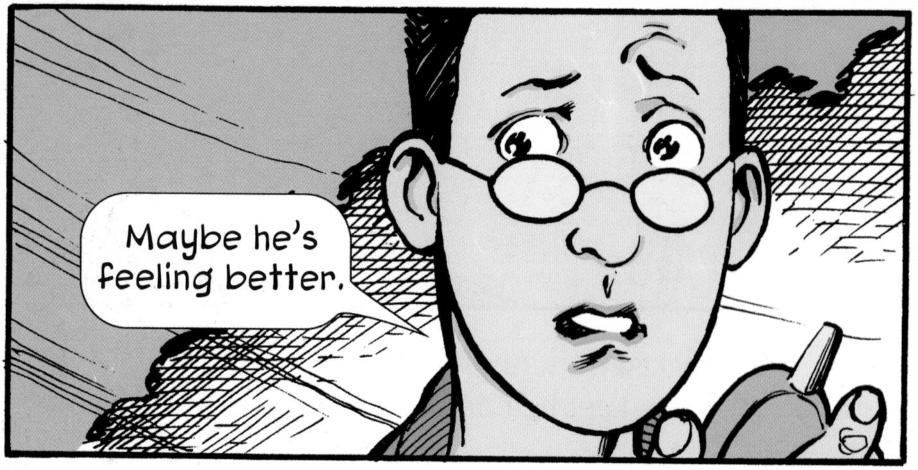
Maybe he's feeling better.

With his fingers trembling, Will punched the buttons. Suddenly the phone went dead. There was no signal.

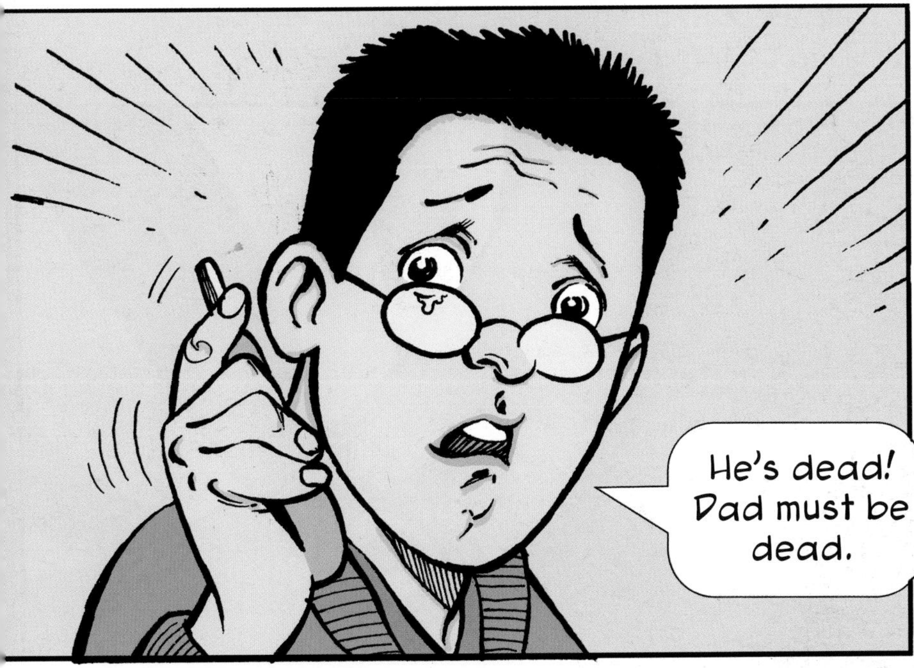
He's dead! Dad must be dead.

"Don't talk stupid," said Steve. His voice was shaky.

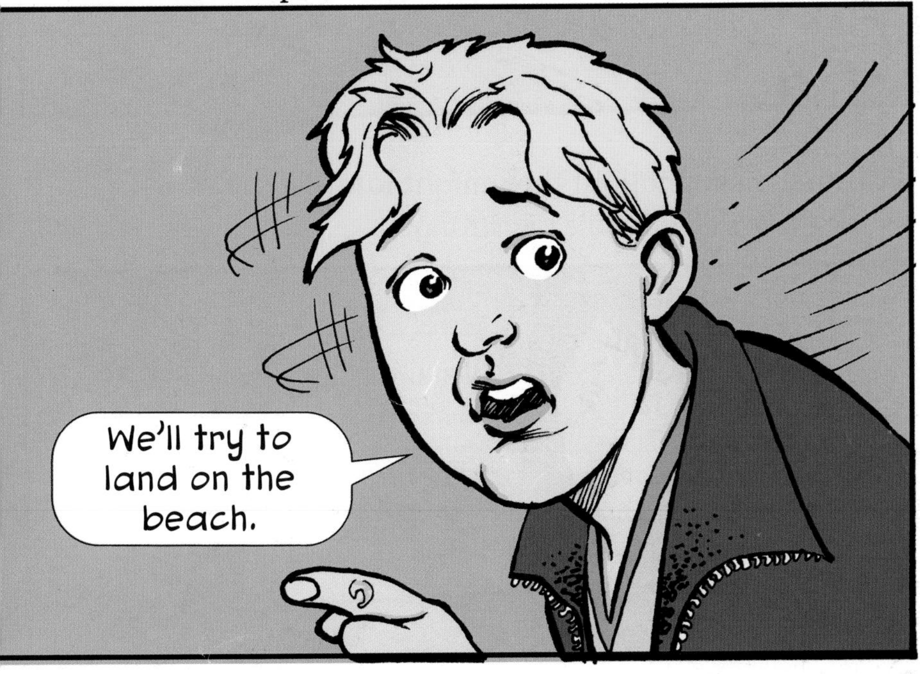
We'll try to land on the beach.

Steve wasn't sure what to do. The beach wasn't very wide. He shut down the burner. Slowly, the balloon began to drift down again.

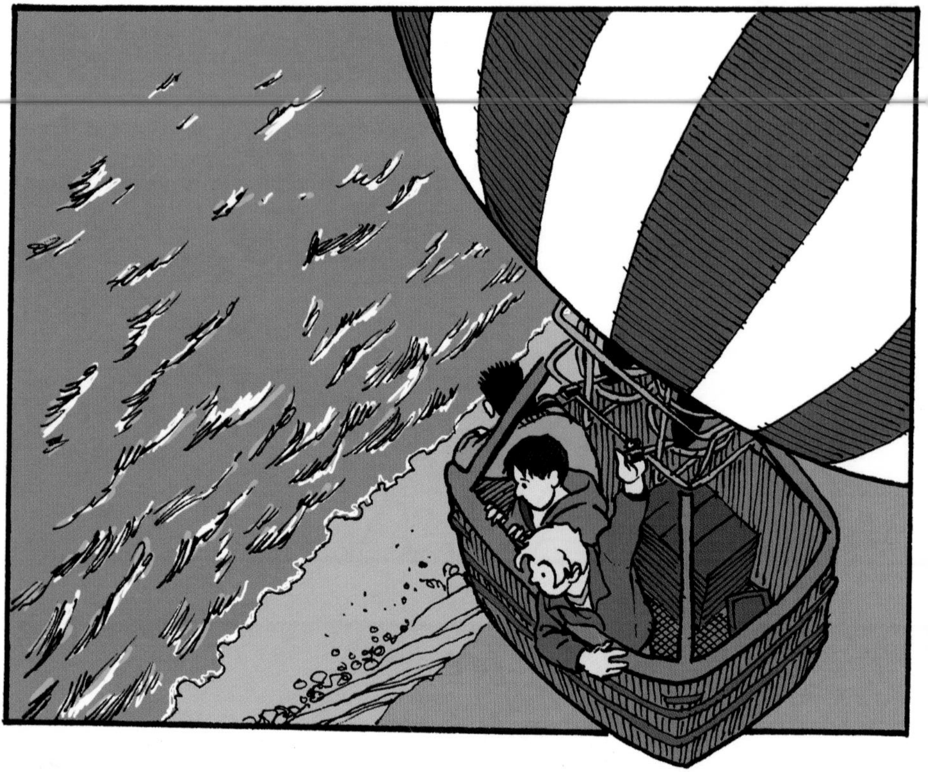

At first Steve thought they might land on the beach, but the wind was still too strong.

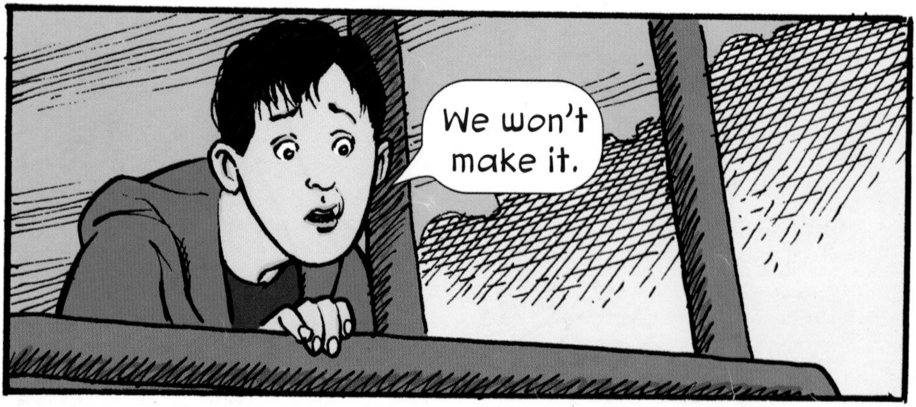
We won't make it.

Then Steve saw the flashing lights of a police car and ambulance speeding along the cliff road.

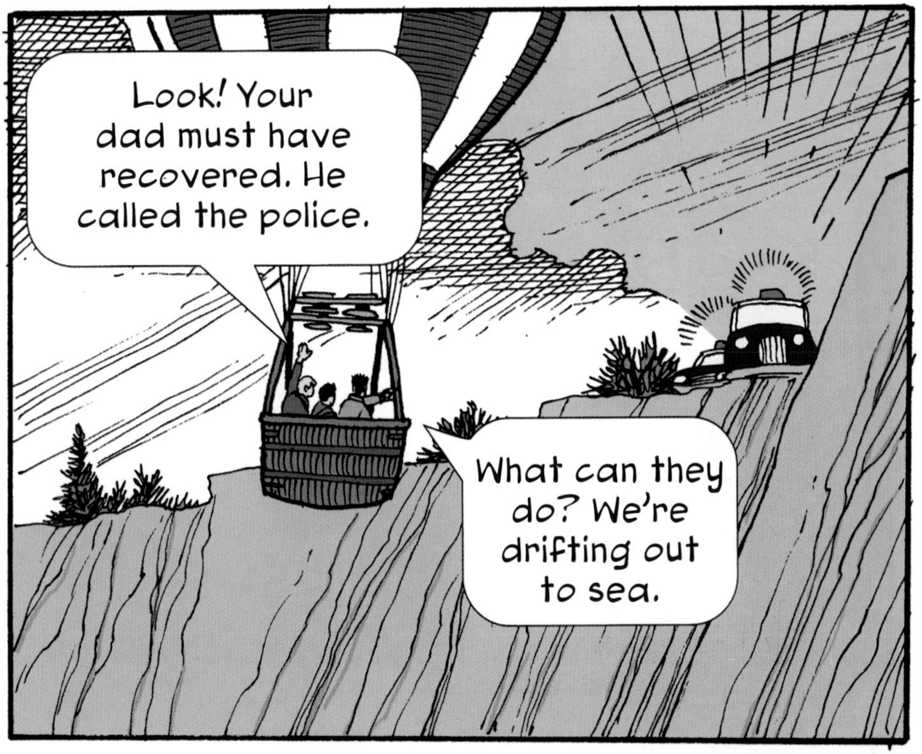
Look! Your dad must have recovered. He called the police.
What can they do? We're drifting out to sea.

Will was panicking. Steve tried to calm him down.

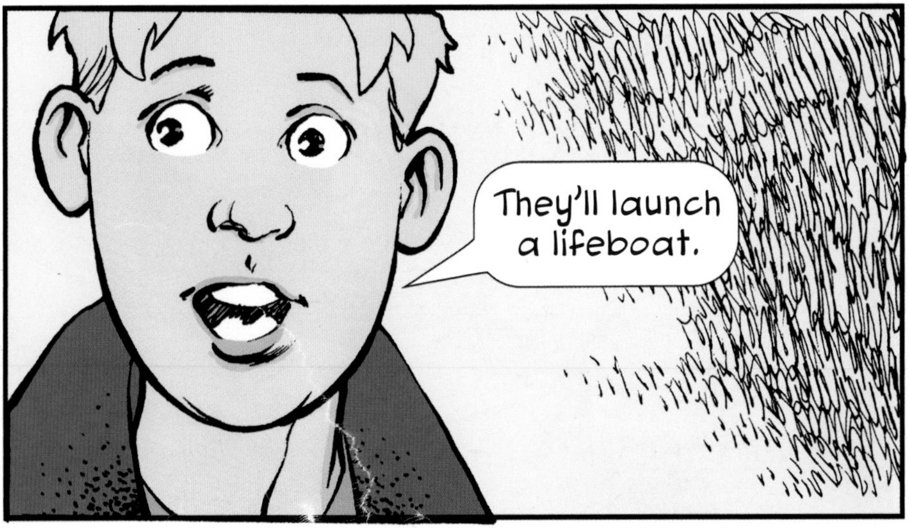
They'll launch a lifeboat.

Steve didn't want the twins to worry, but he was beginning to feel sick.

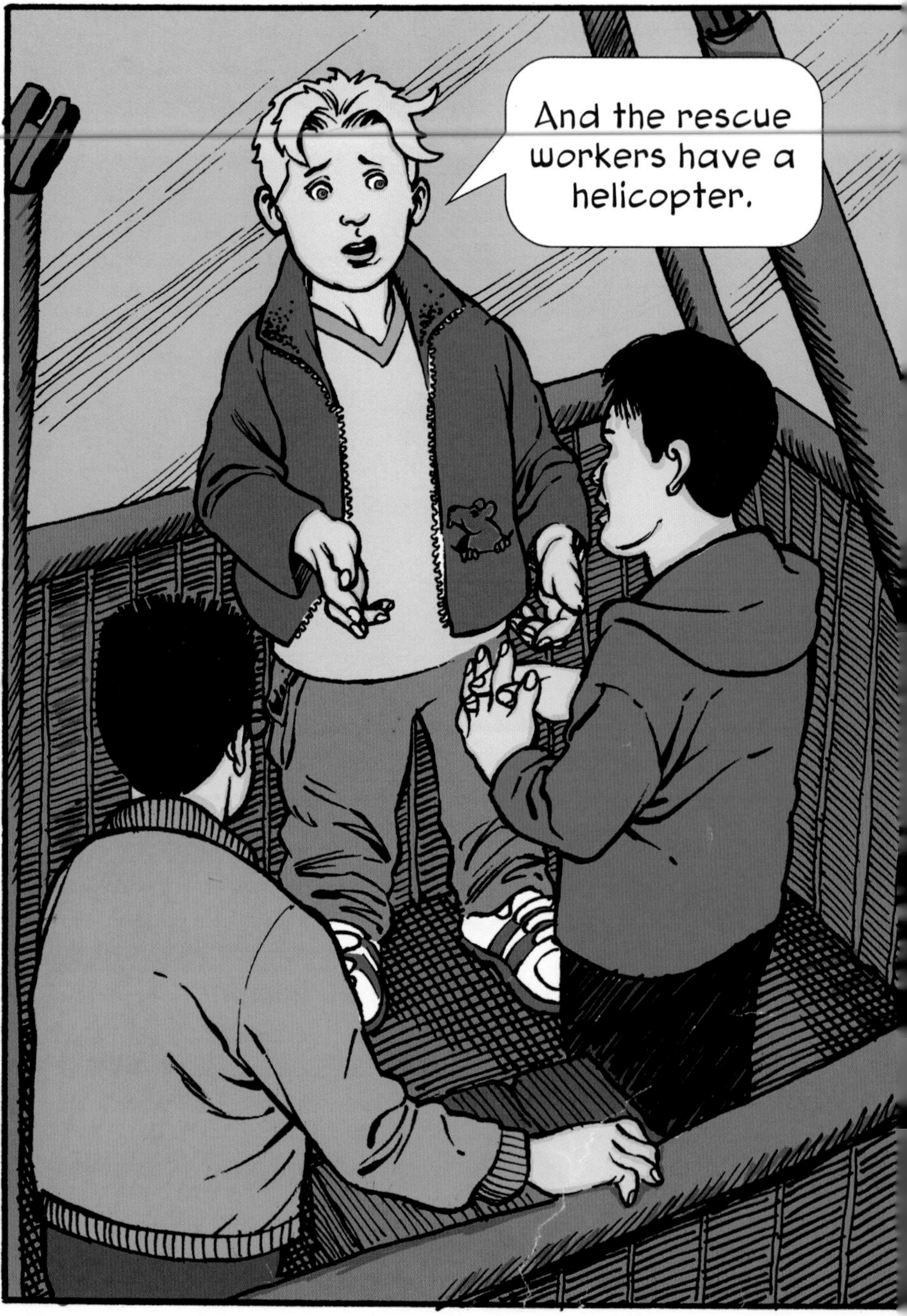
And the rescue workers have a helicopter.

The balloon was past the beach now, and they were out over the sea. The waves were crashing violently below them.

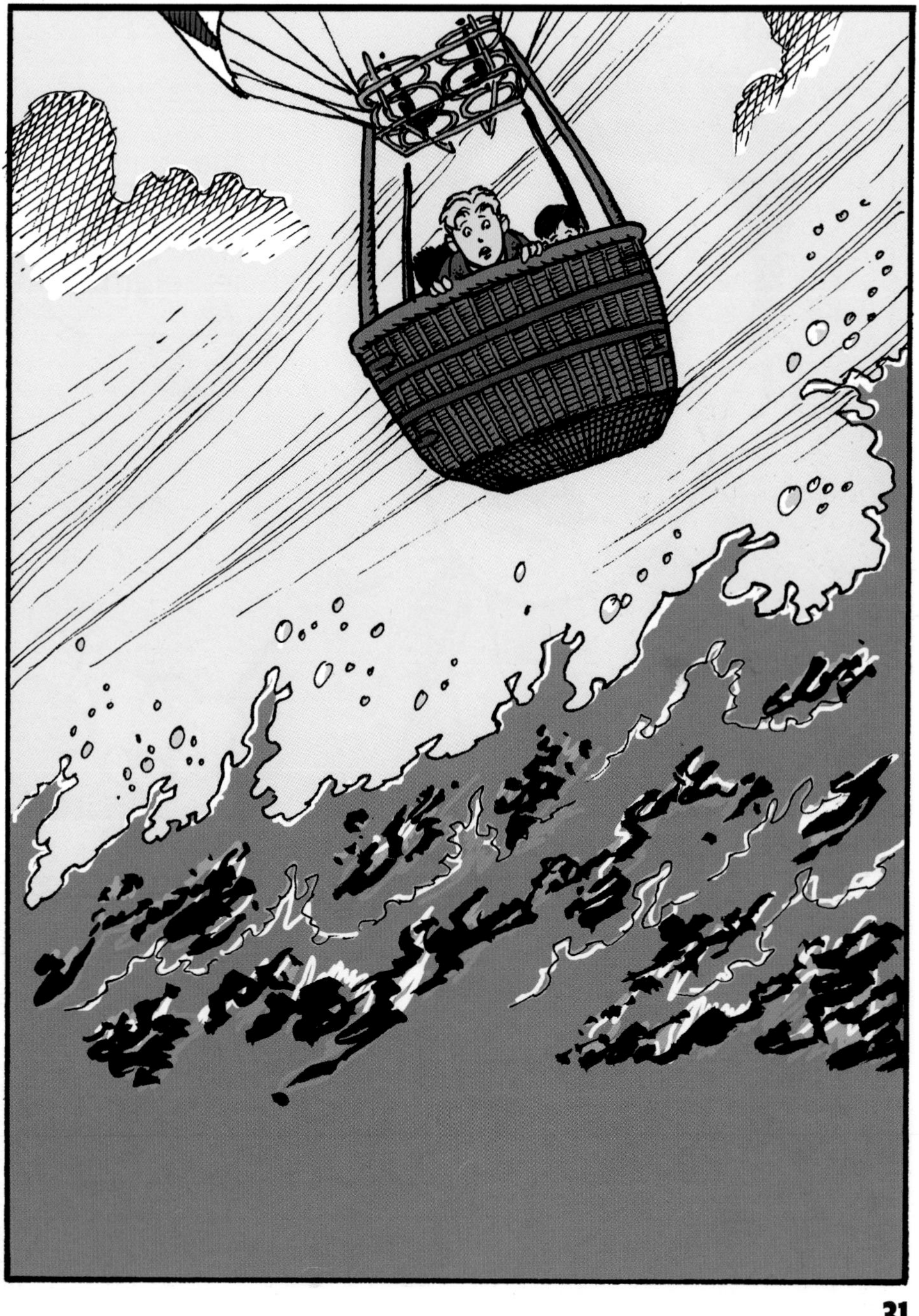

Chapter Four

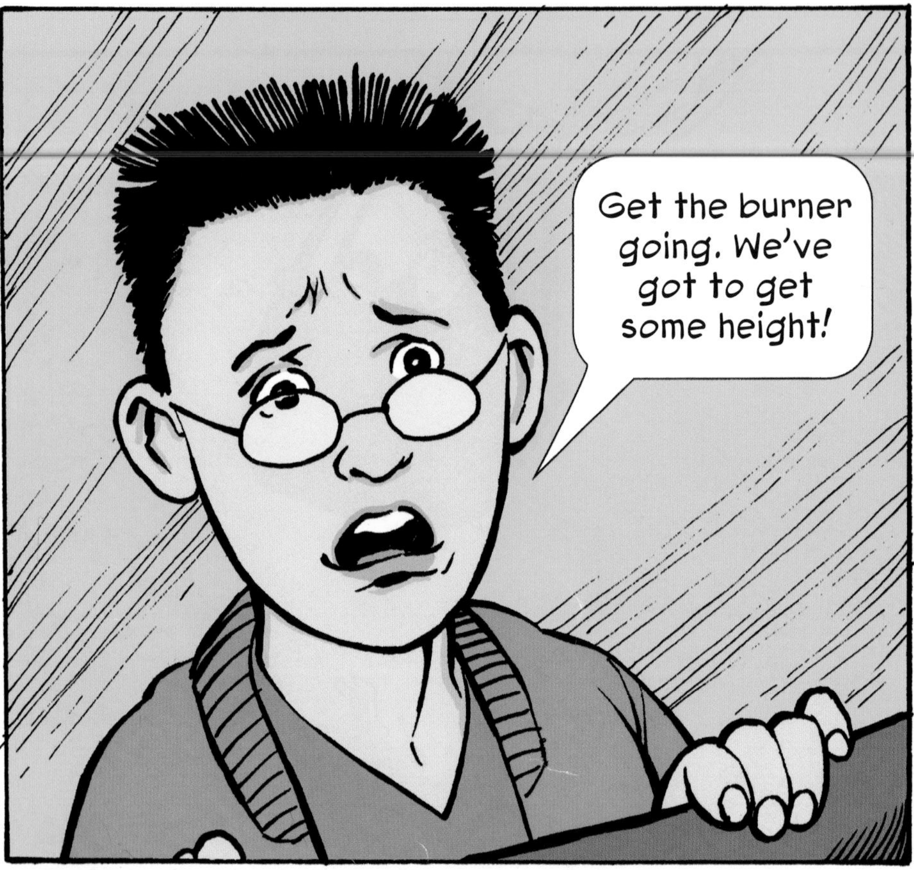
Get the burner going. We've got to get some height!

Steve was just about to grab the rod again.

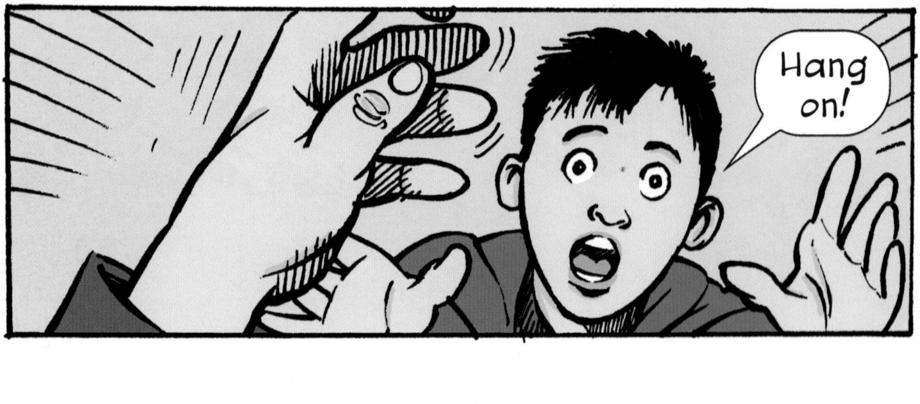
Hang on!

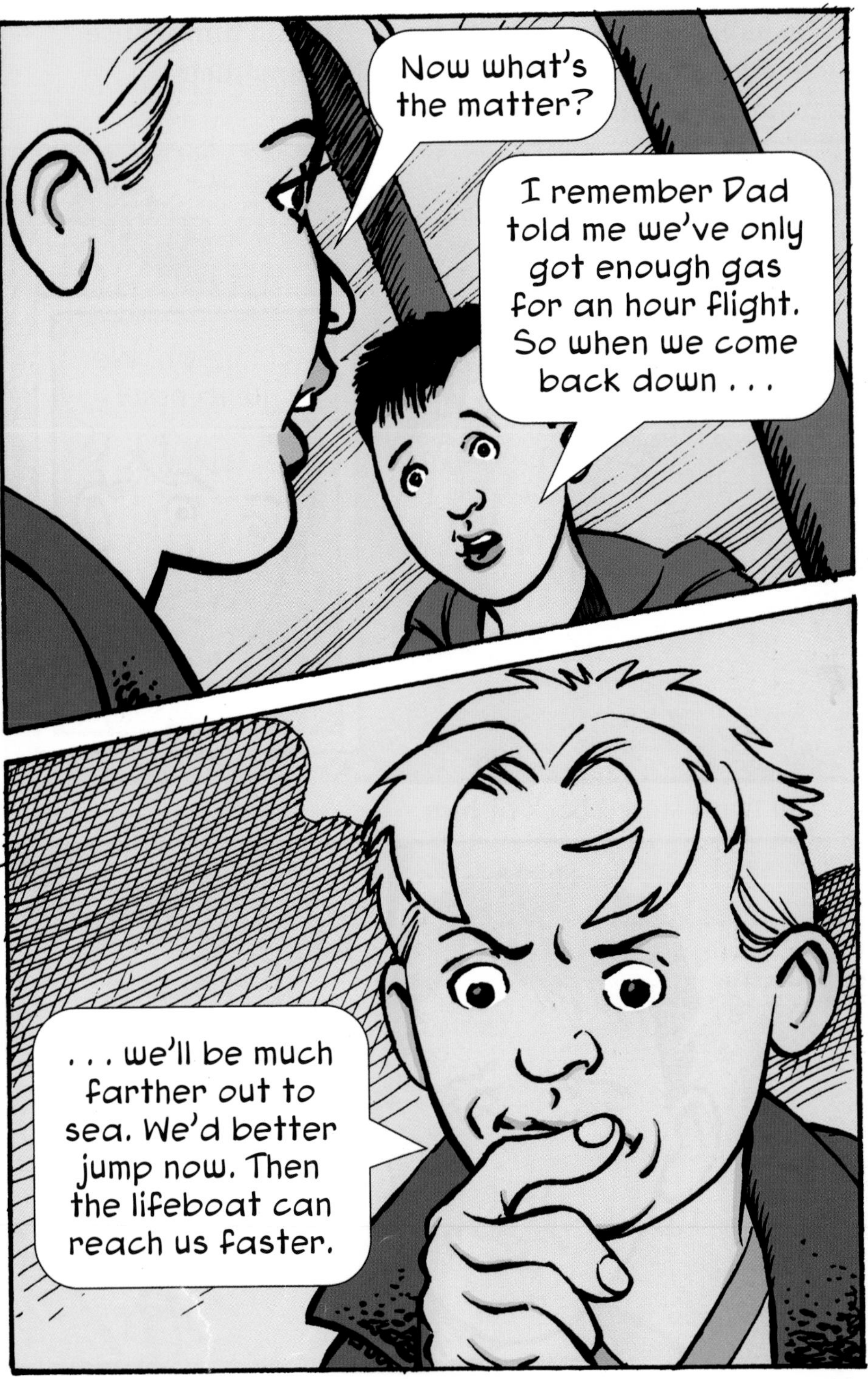
Now what's the matter?
I remember Dad told me we've only got enough gas for an hour flight. So when we come back down . . .
. . . we'll be much farther out to sea. We'd better jump now. Then the lifeboat can reach us faster.

He glanced back to see the police car and ambulance on the top of the cliff. They were flashing their headlights at the drifting balloon.

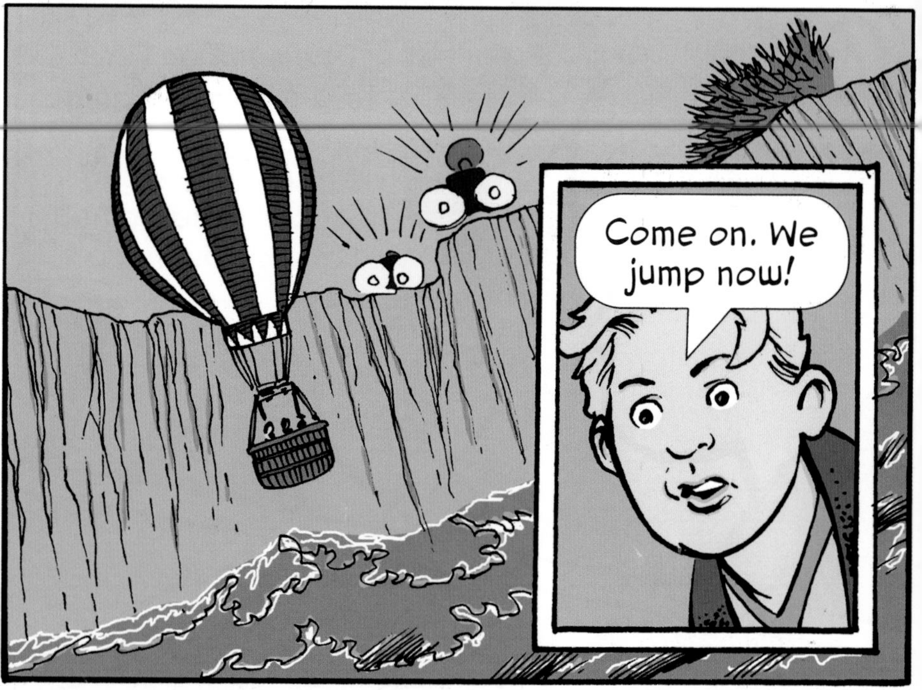
Come on. We jump now!

The twins stared back at him.

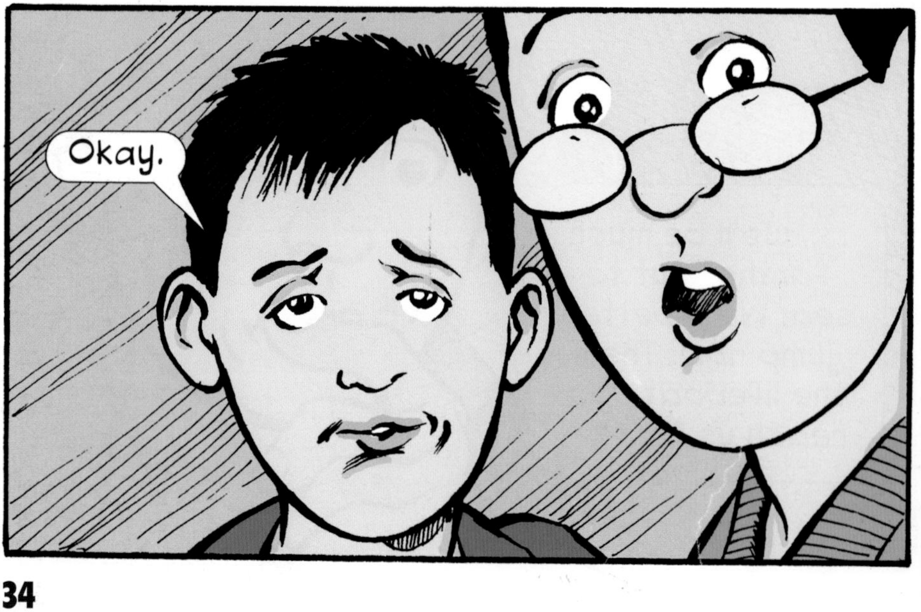
Okay.

Steve began to worry about Buster, who was still squirming in his pocket and squeaking sadly. He'd been his pet for a year and they did everything together. How could he keep Buster safe?

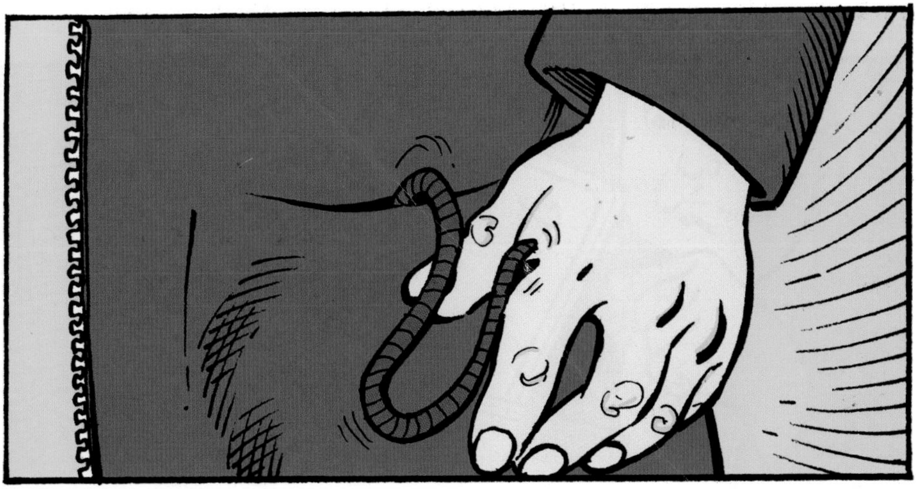

Then he had an idea. Lying in the basket was Steve's sandwich box.

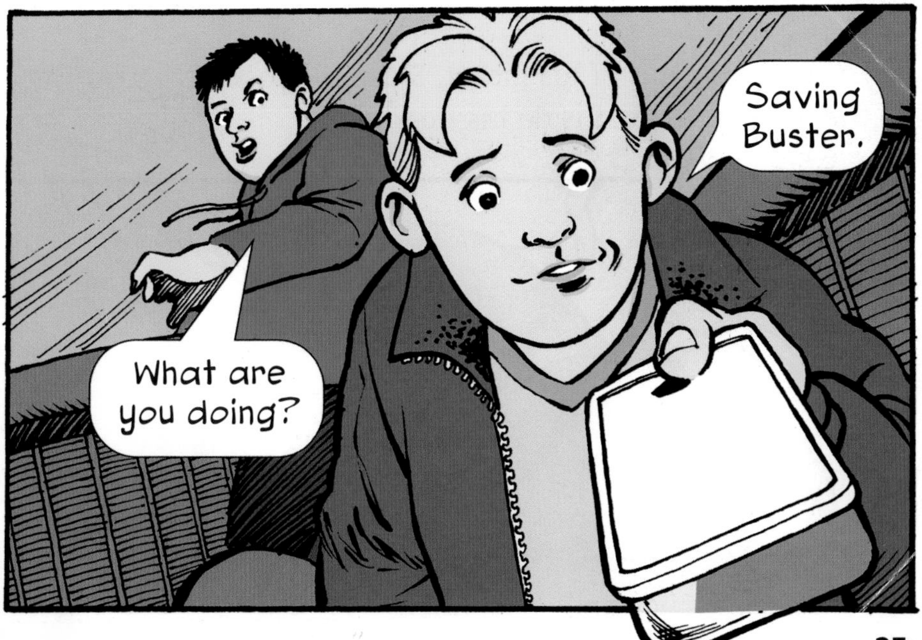
Saving Buster.
What are you doing?

Steve pulled out the struggling white rat and dumped him in the box. Then he took out his penknife and punched six small holes in the lid. Steve figured the holes would allow Buster to breathe without letting in too much water.

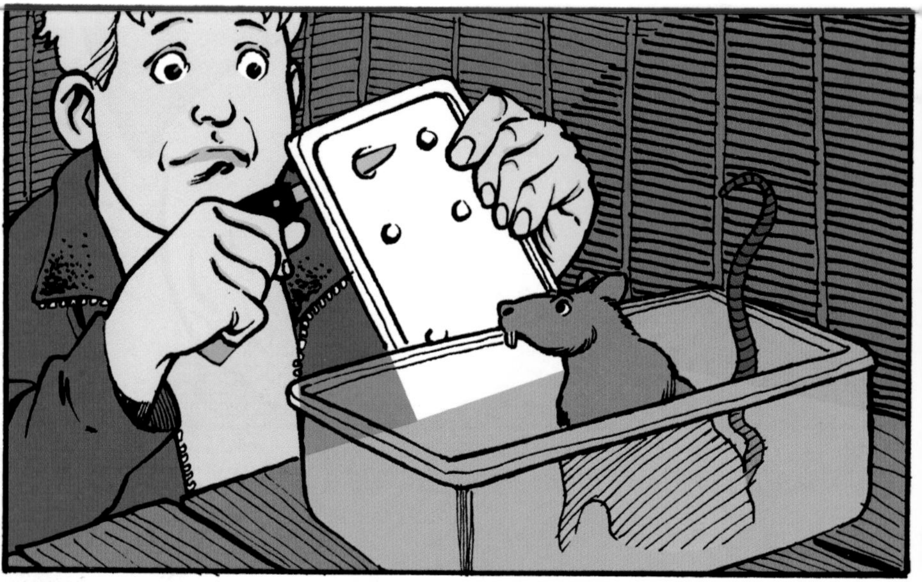

Using the strings of his jacket, Steve managed to strap the sandwich box inside his hood.

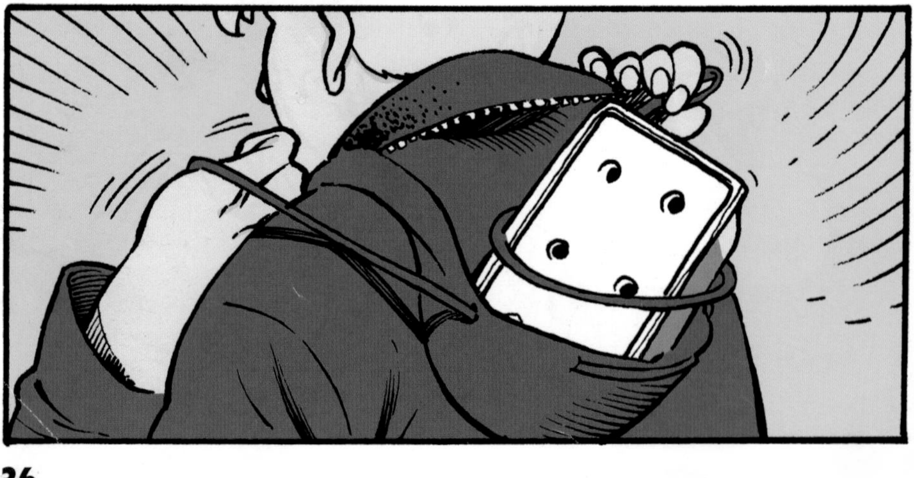

When Steve looked down again, he saw the balloon was much closer to the angry sea.

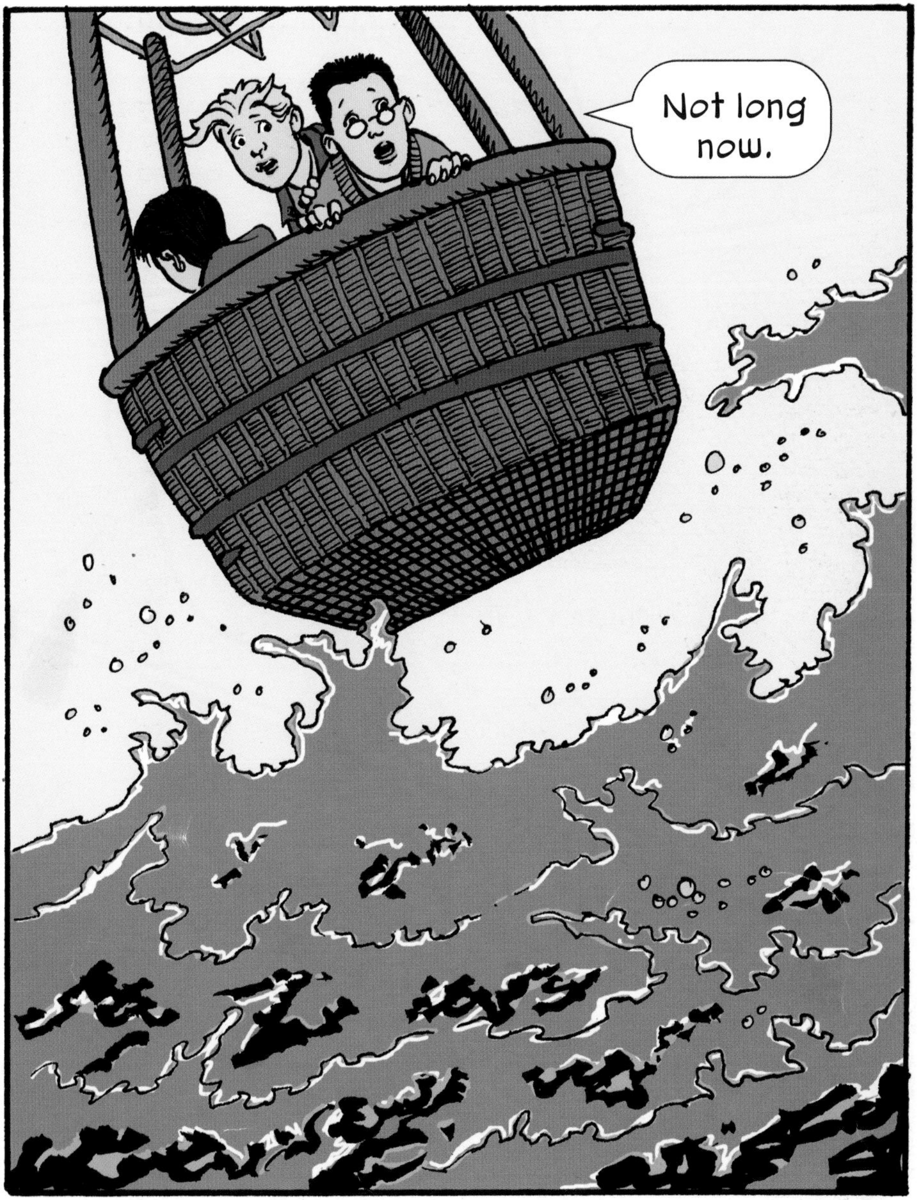
Not long now.

Then Will remembered something important.

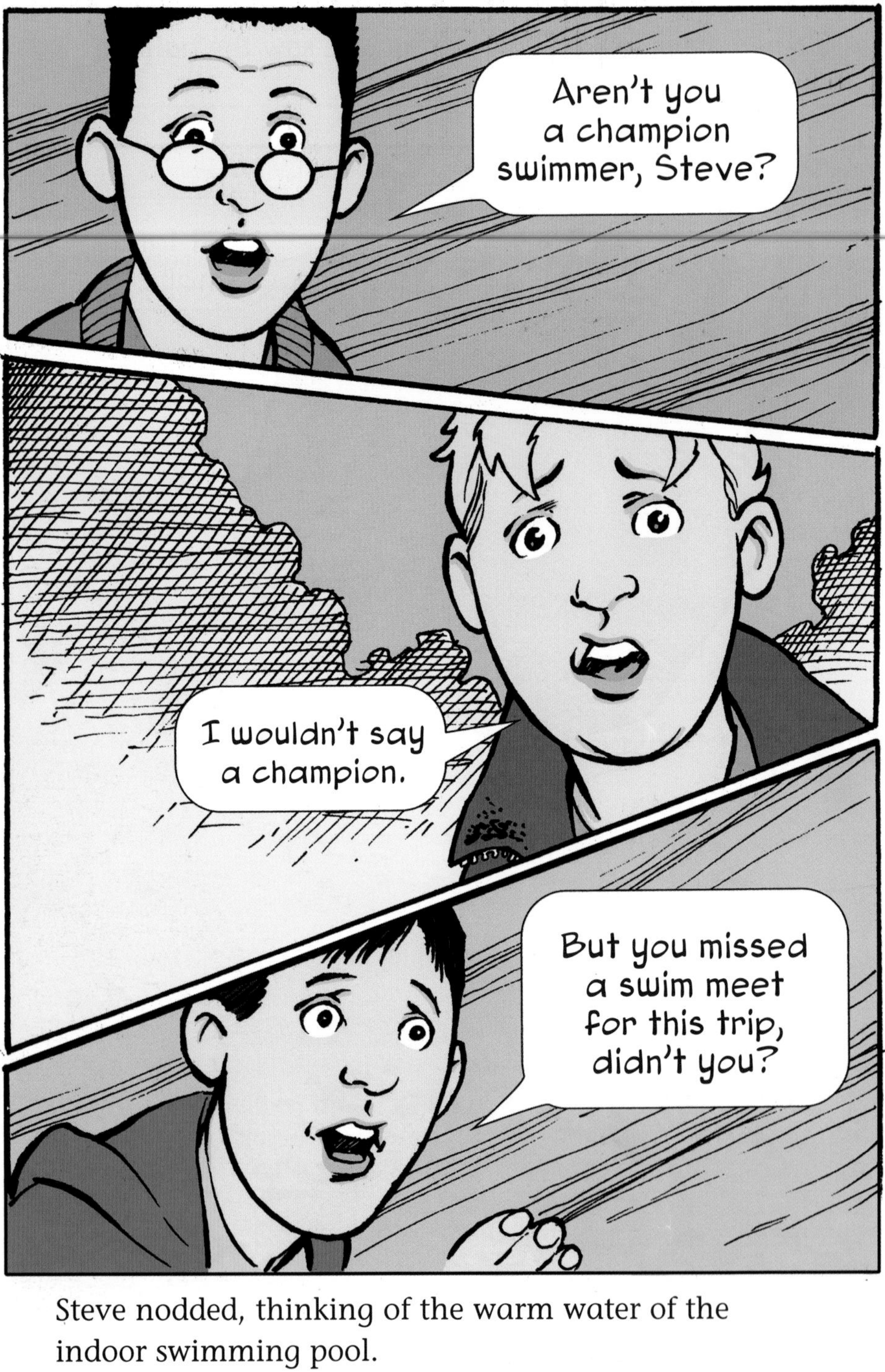
Aren't you a champion swimmer, Steve?
I wouldn't say a champion.
But you missed a swim meet for this trip, didn't you?

Steve nodded, thinking of the warm water of the indoor swimming pool.

Cold spray from a huge rolling wave hit him in the face. He shivered miserably.

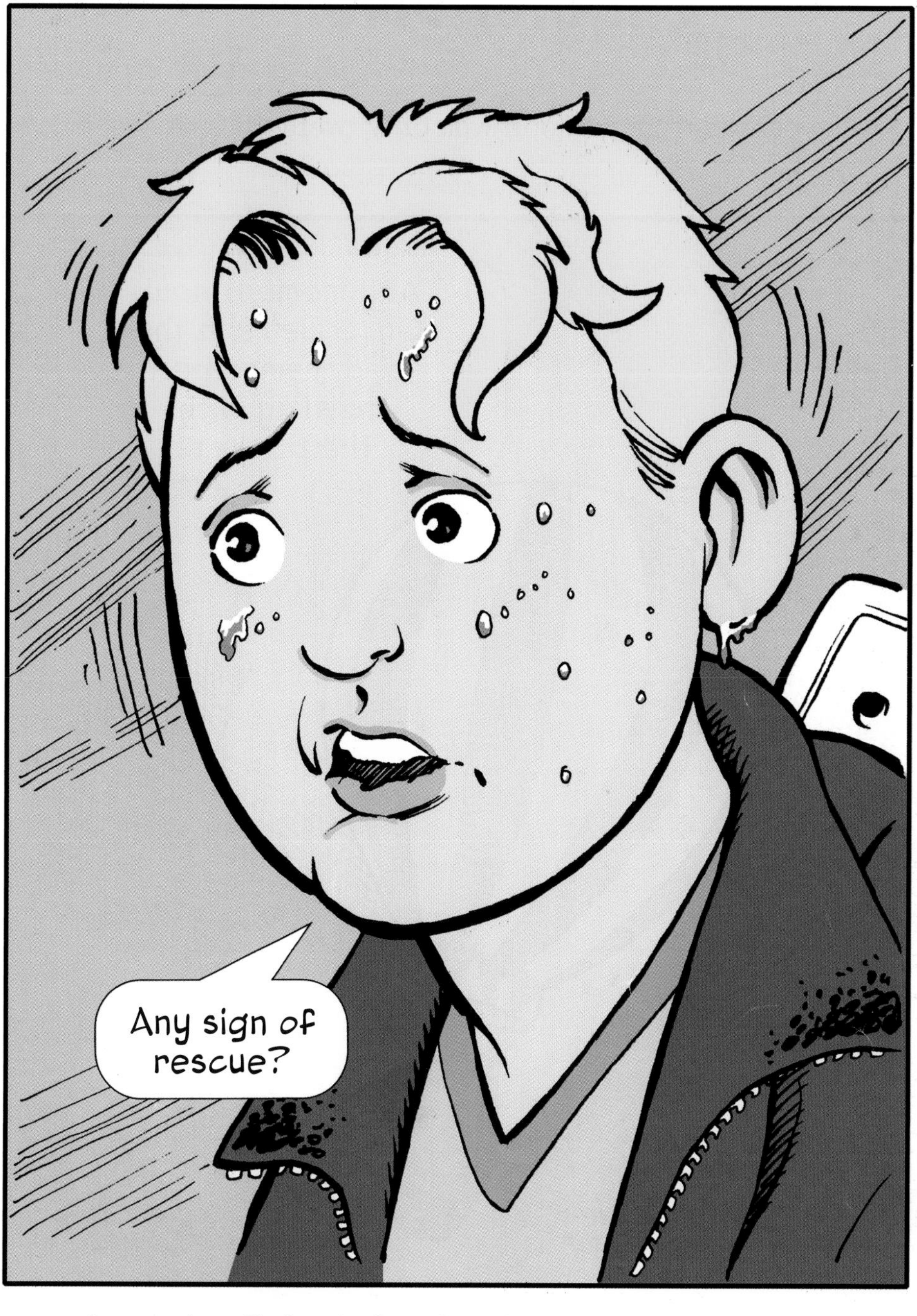
Any sign of rescue?

Joe and Will shook their heads.

Chapter Five

Steve figured the balloon was only twenty feet above the waves.

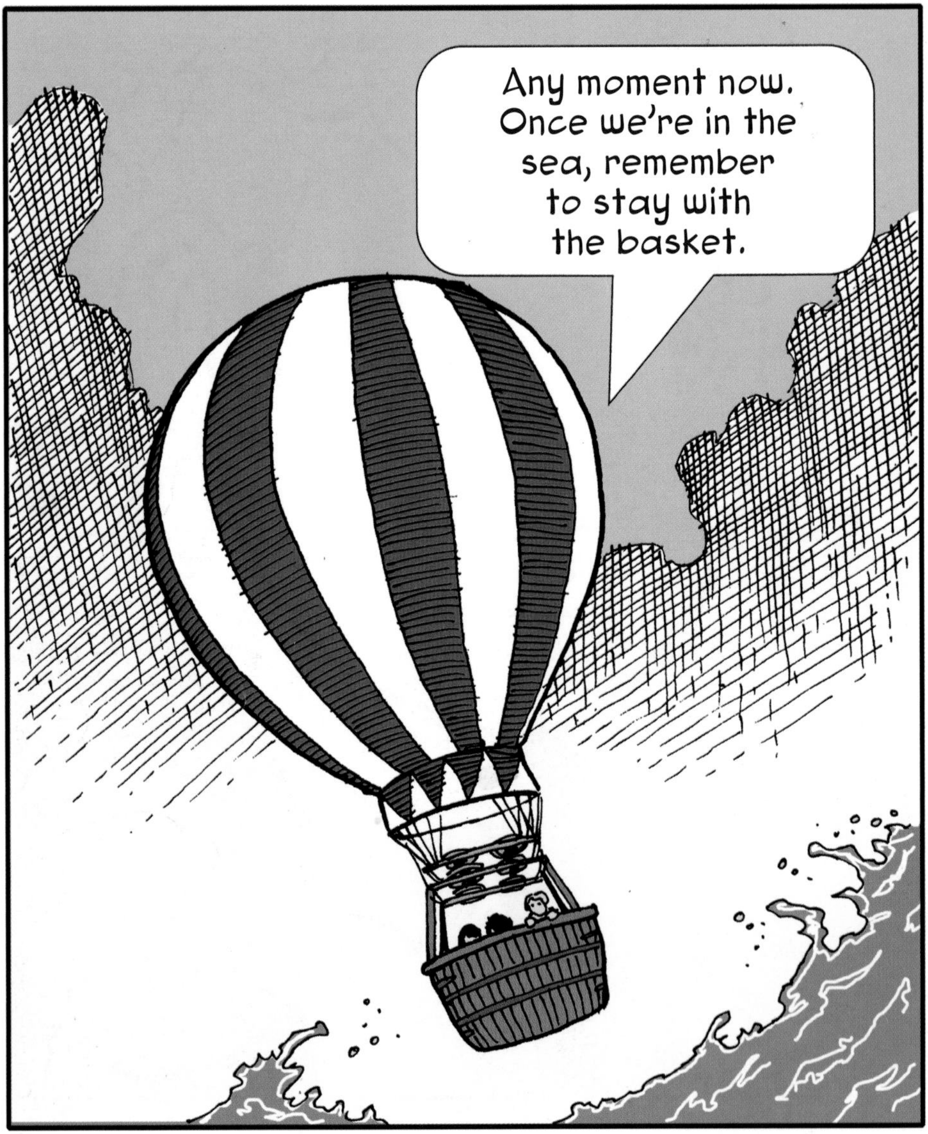
Any moment now. Once we're in the sea, remember to stay with the basket.

Steve's stomach was churning like the waves as he checked the horizon. Where was the stupid lifeboat? There was a clap of thunder and then the rain came down, hard and strong, hitting the waves.

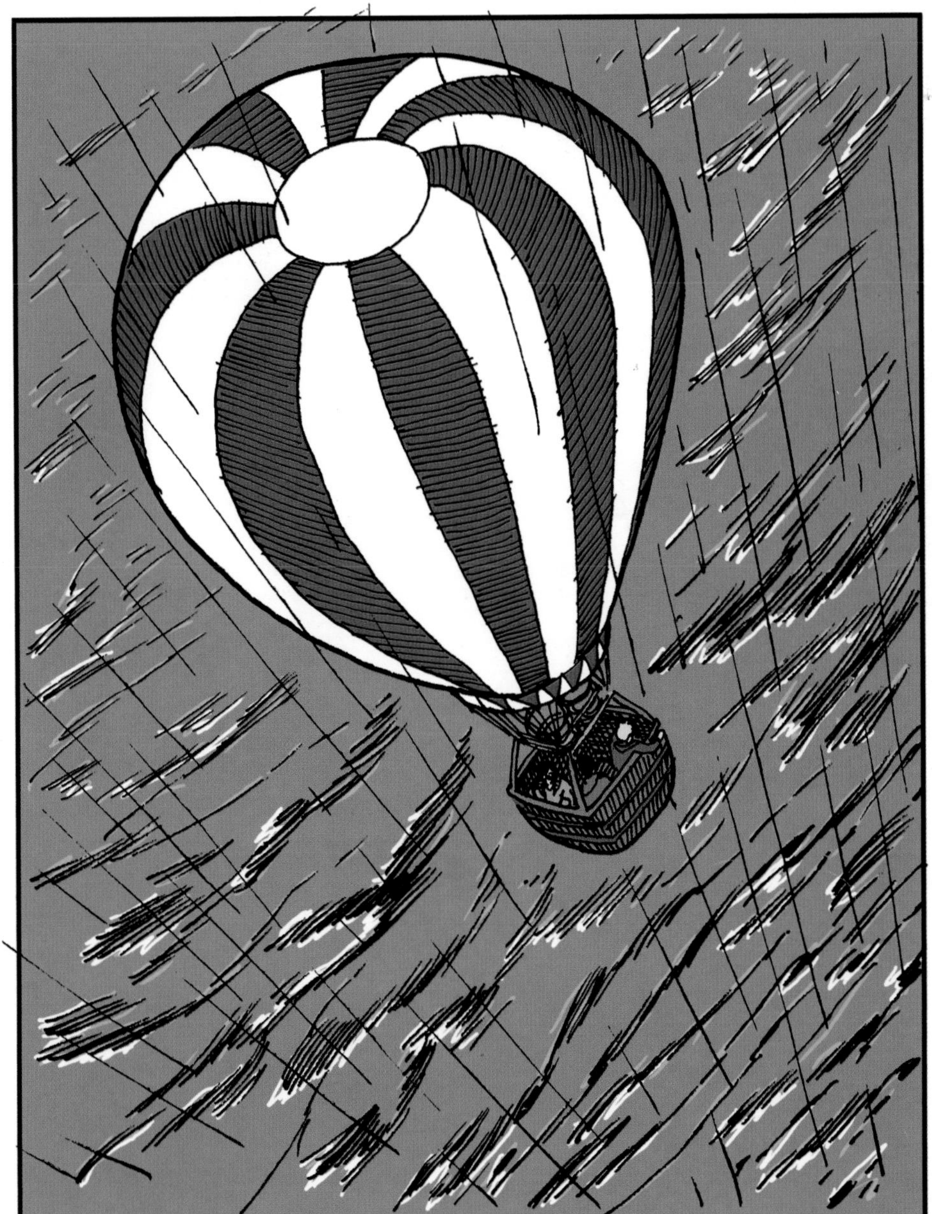

Steve had another thought.

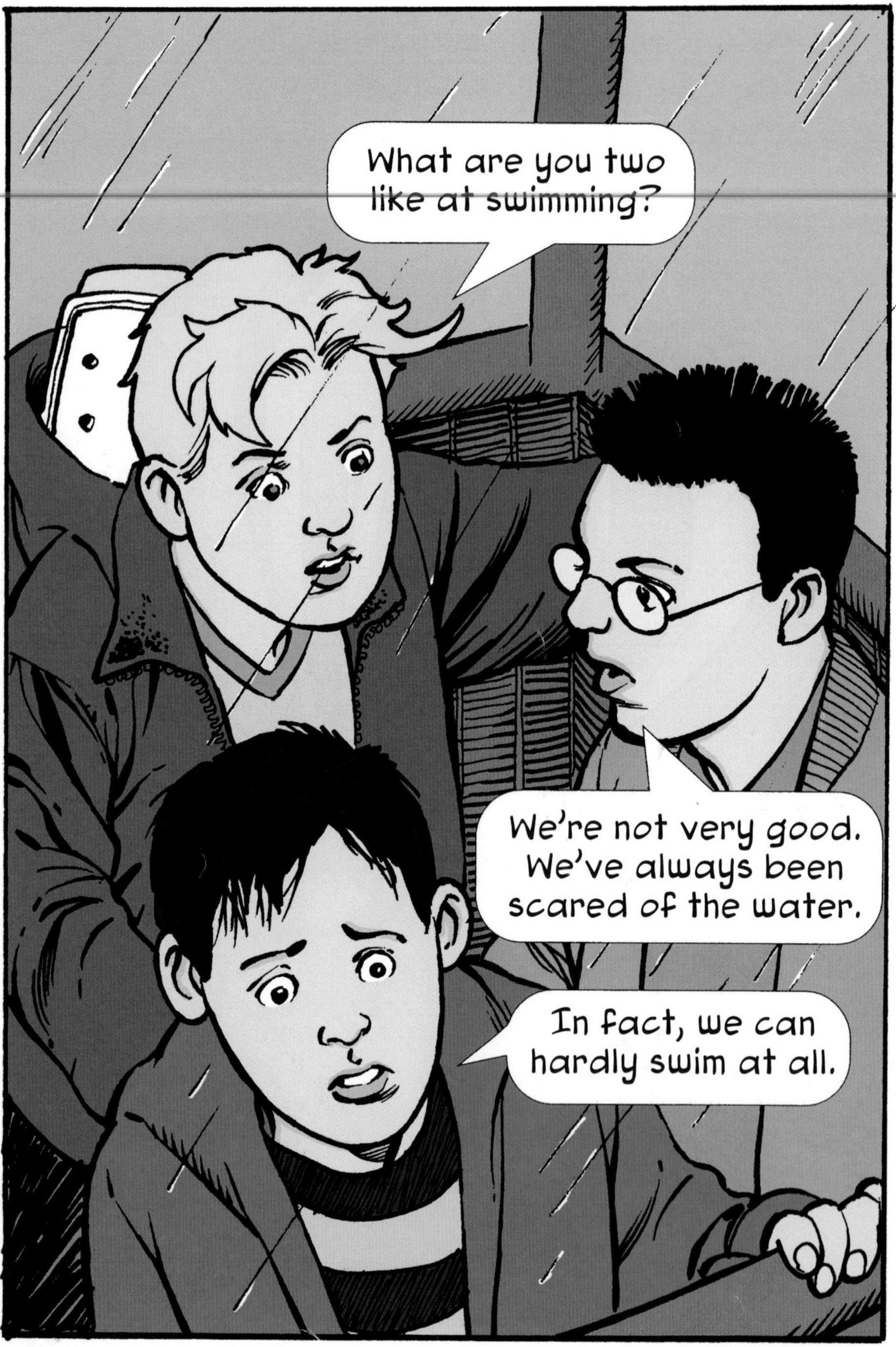
What are you two like at swimming?
We're not very good. We've always been scared of the water.
In fact, we can hardly swim at all.

Steve's heart pounded. How was he going to save Will, Joe, and Buster? The basket was skimming the surface now and they were already soaked by spray.

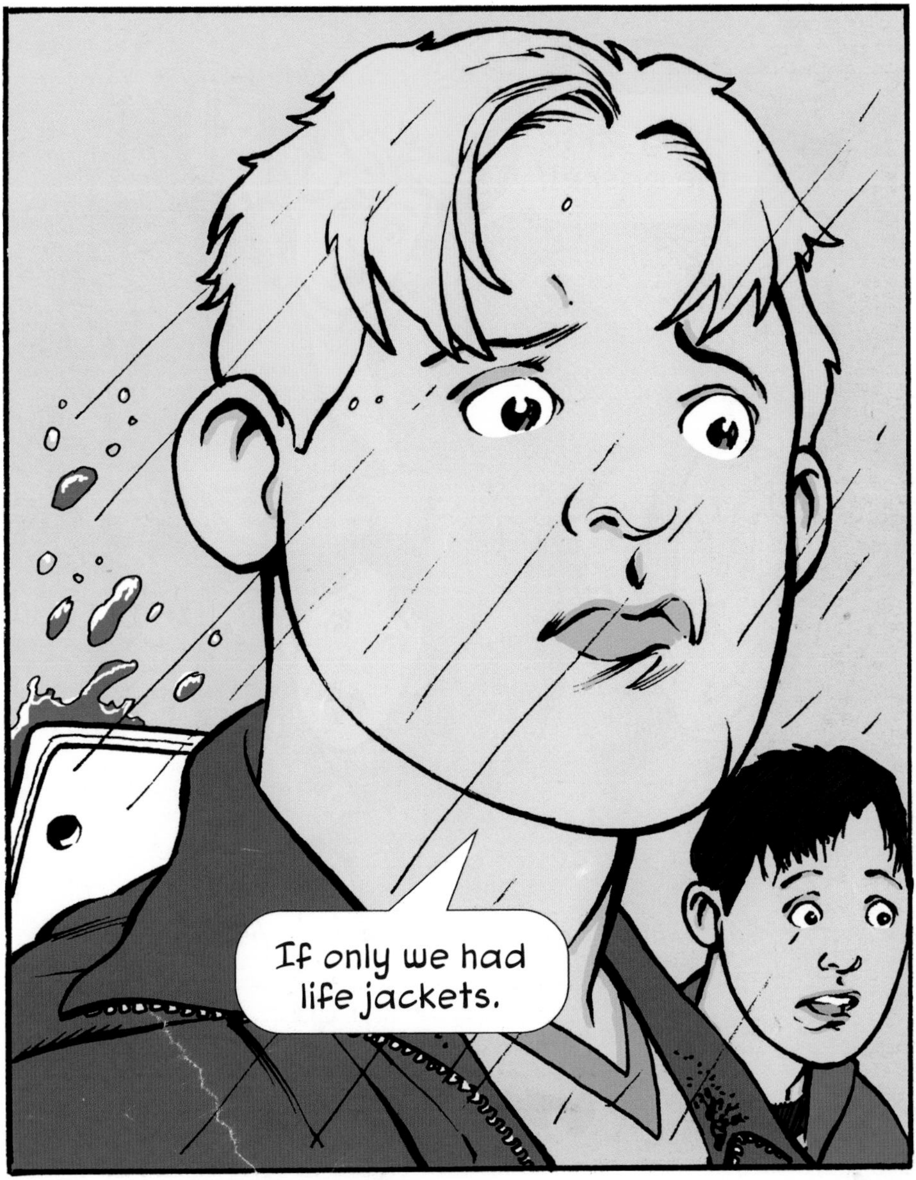
If only we had life jackets.

The basket hit the waves and turned on its side, throwing them into the sea. Then the balloon itself collapsed, spreading out over the waves.

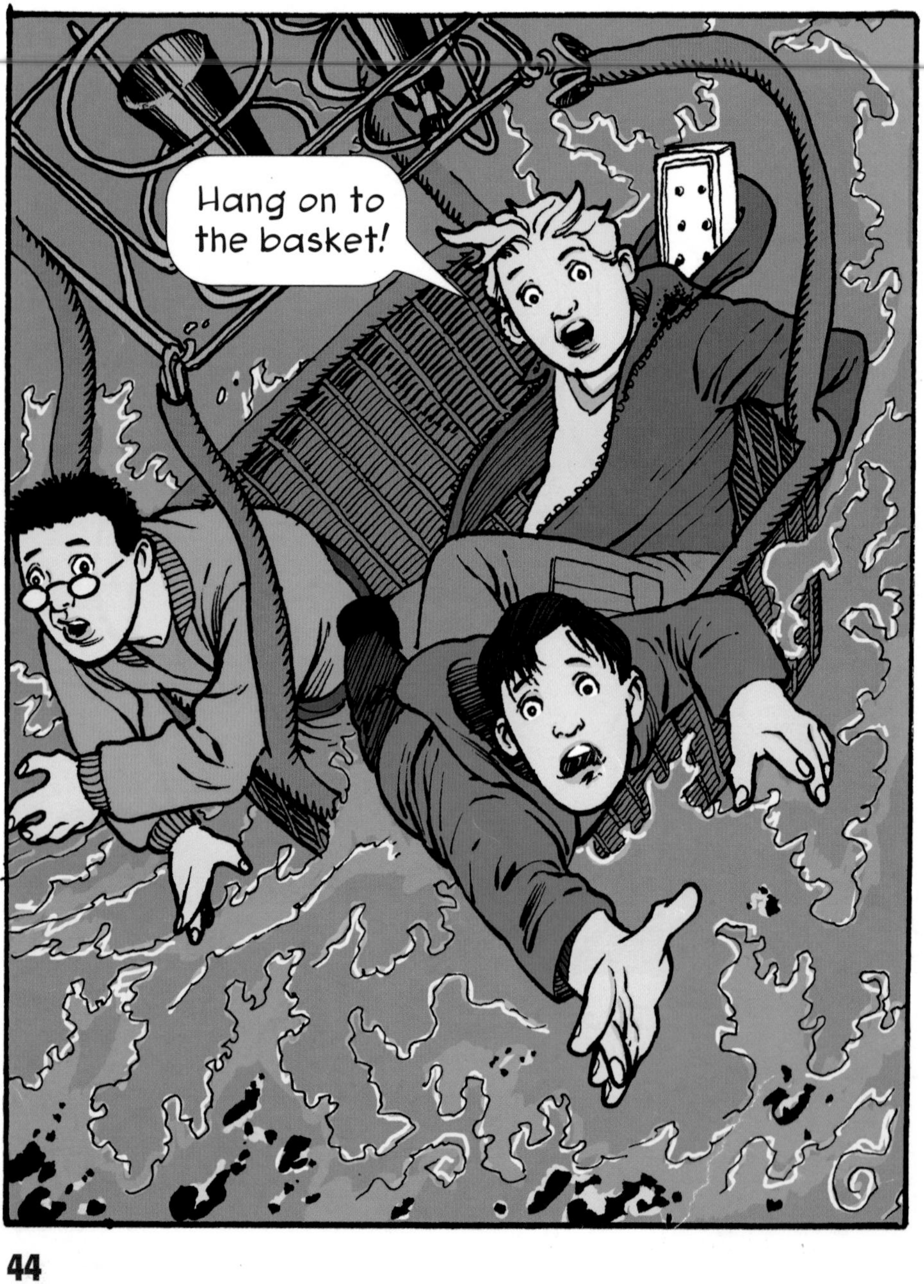
Hang on to the basket!

Steve held his head as high as he could to keep Buster's box clear of the water.

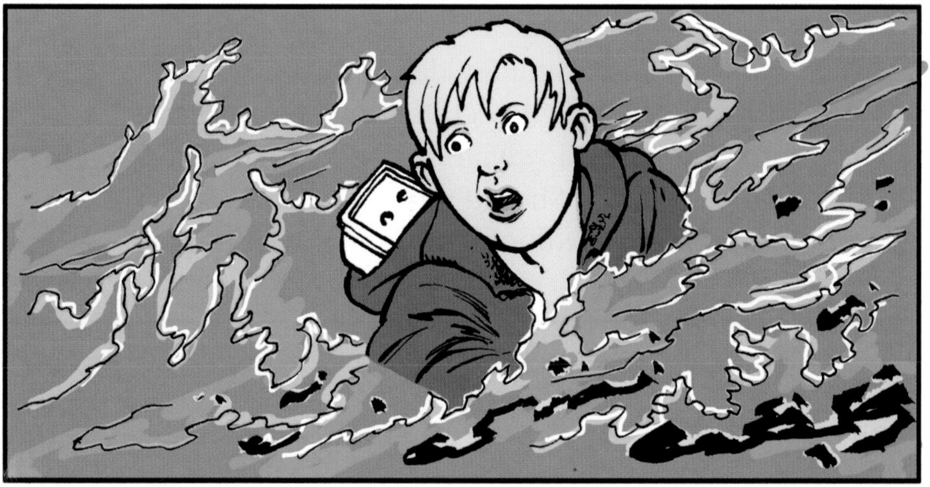

He clung to the basket which was now tipped on its side, sinking into the sea.

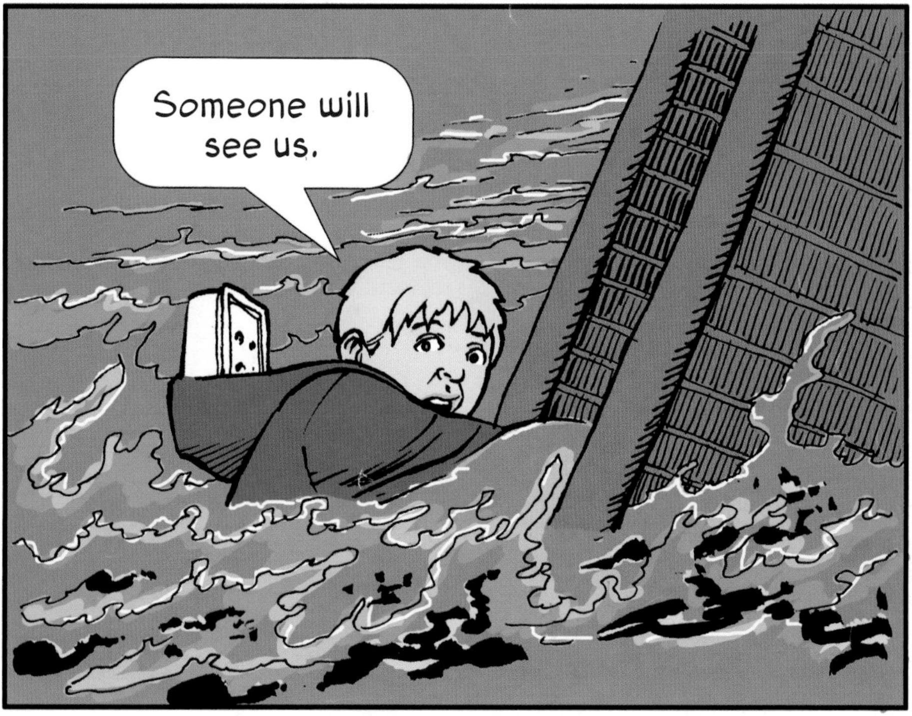
Someone will see us.

But neither twin replied.

Chapter Six

Fear swept through him. Suddenly Steve saw Will struggling, but unable to get back to the basket. Steve swam towards him slowly, trying to keep his head up to protect Buster. Should he dump him? Wasn't a human life more valuable than a rat's? He had to save Will.

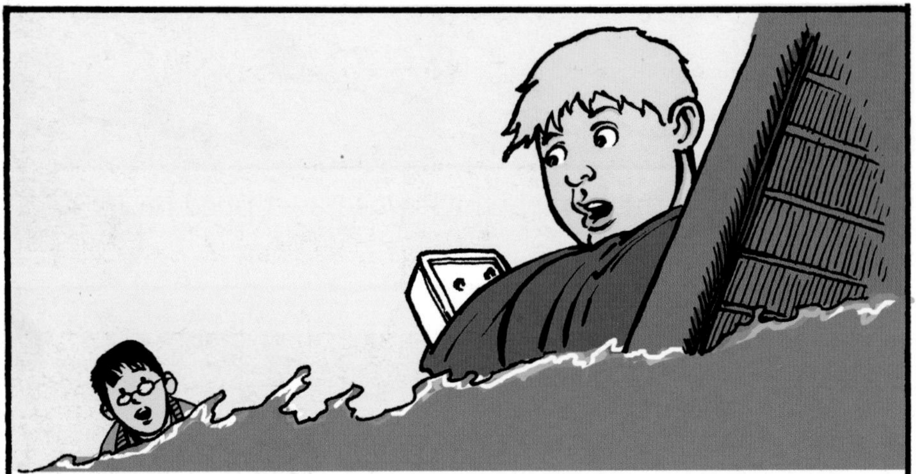

A giant wave broke over him and the box floated free.

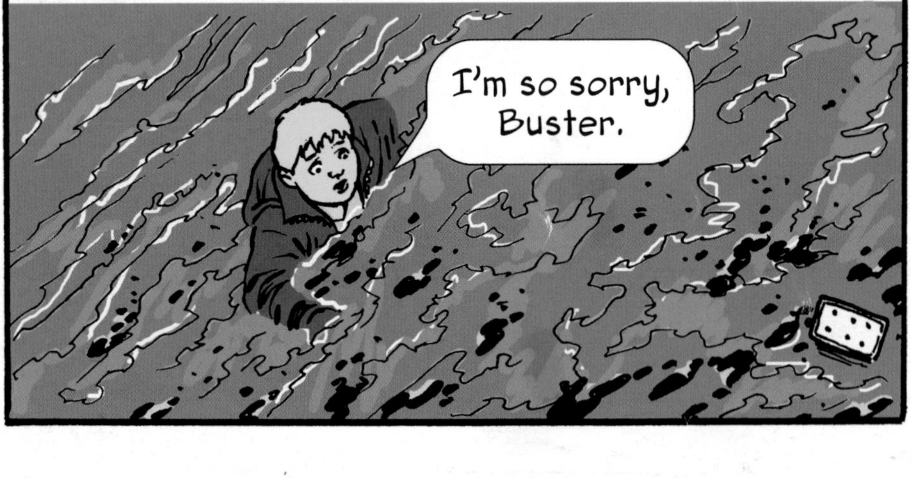
I'm so sorry, Buster.

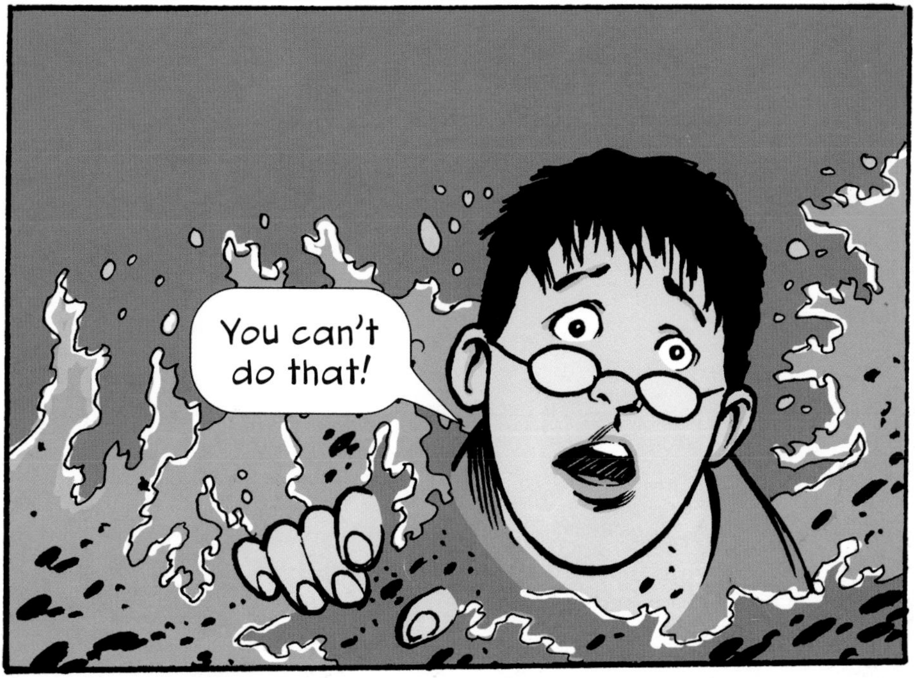
You can't do that!

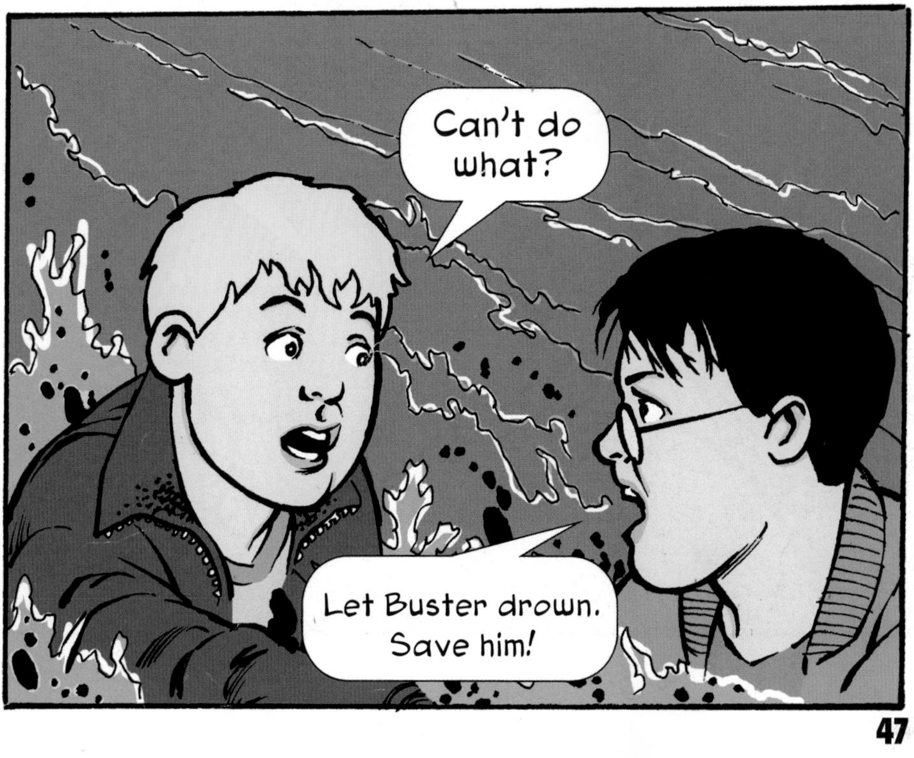
Can't do what?
Let Buster drown. Save him!

Steve grabbed Buster's box again as Will slipped past him and grabbed the basket.

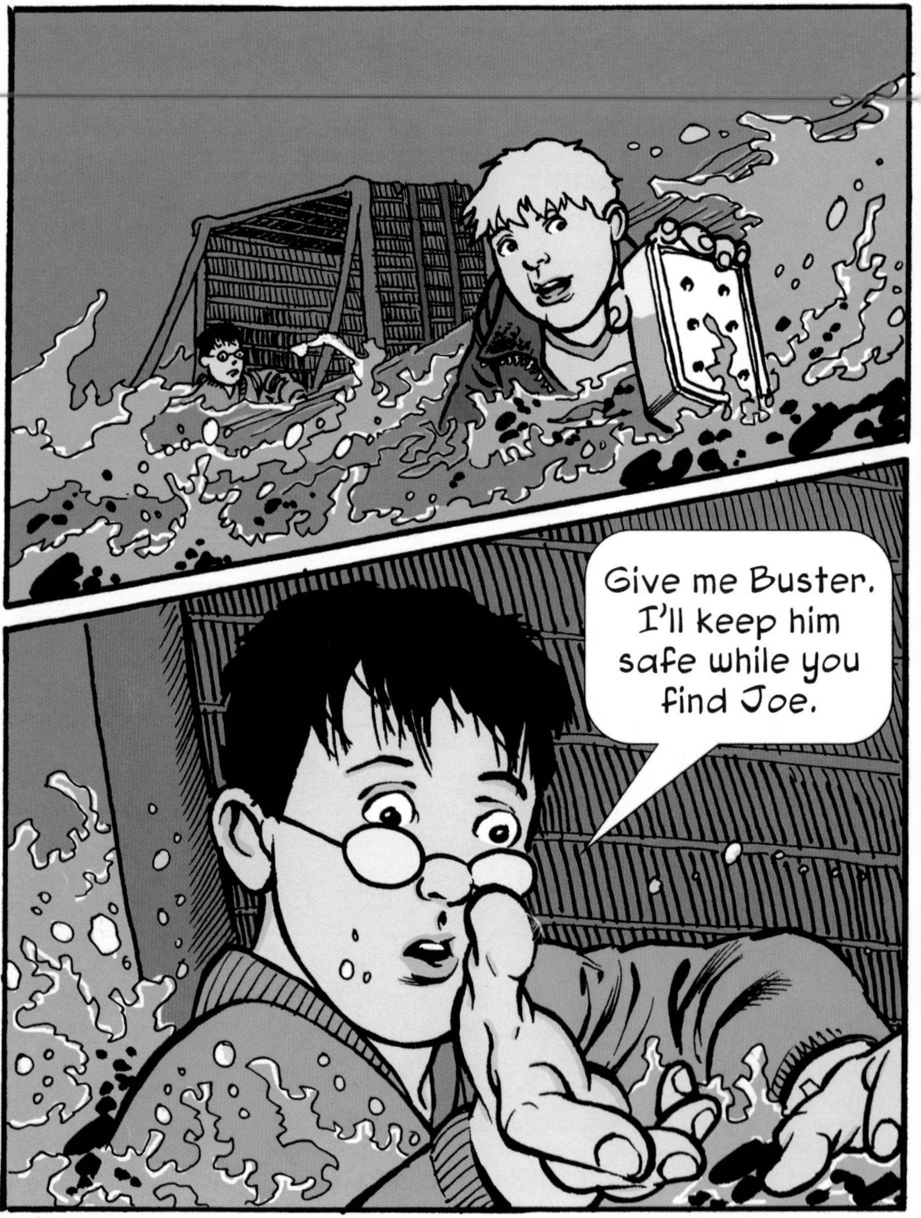
Give me Buster. I'll keep him safe while you find Joe.

Eventually, Steve found Joe floating on his back under the folds of the balloon.

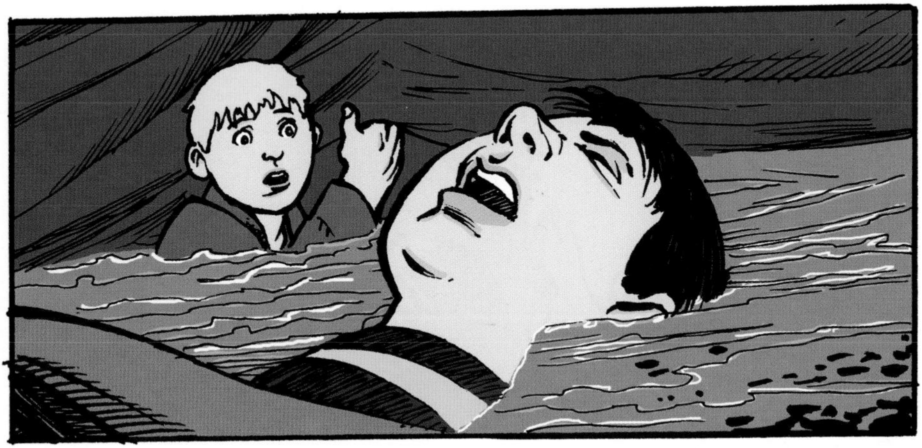

Steve grabbed him in a position that he learned from a lifeguard, but Joe was heavy in his soaked jacket and jeans. Steve could barely keep Joe's head above the waves.

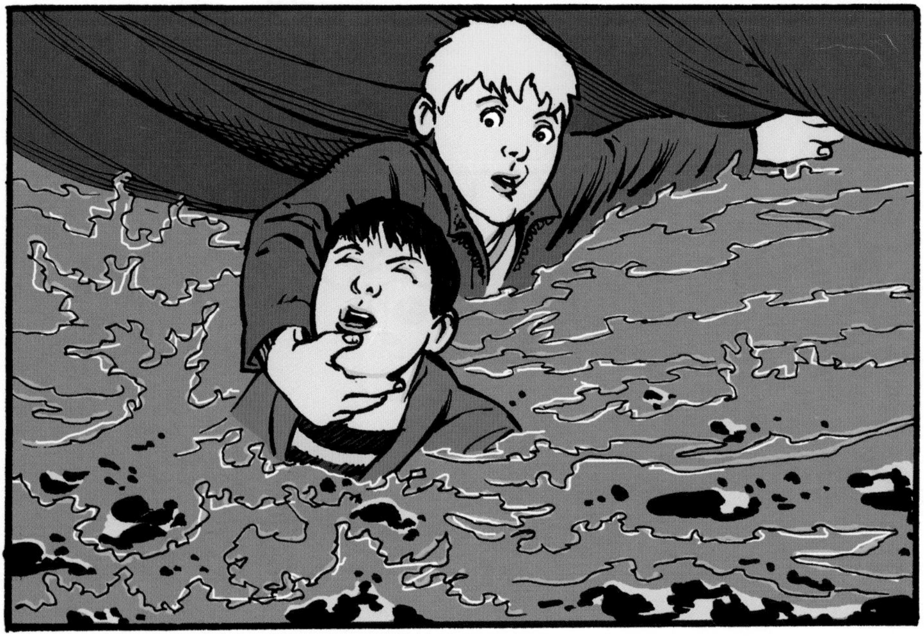

Suddenly, to Steve's relief, Joe began to choke, spewing out water and gasping for air.

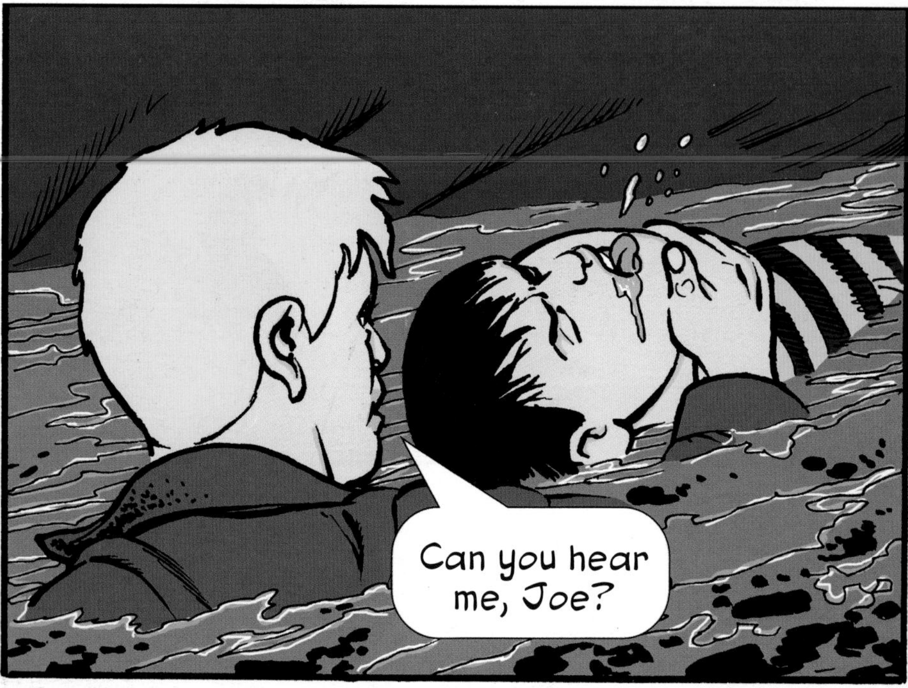
Can you hear me, Joe?

There was no reply.

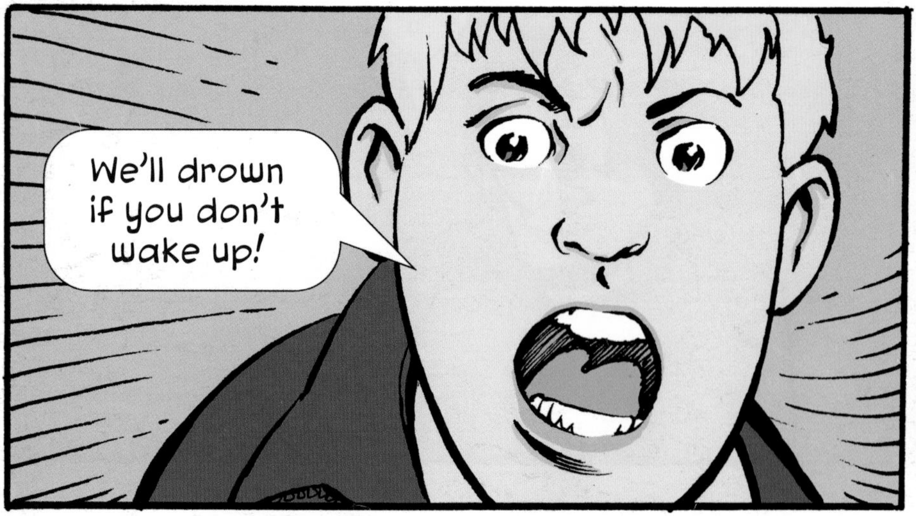
We'll drown if you don't wake up!

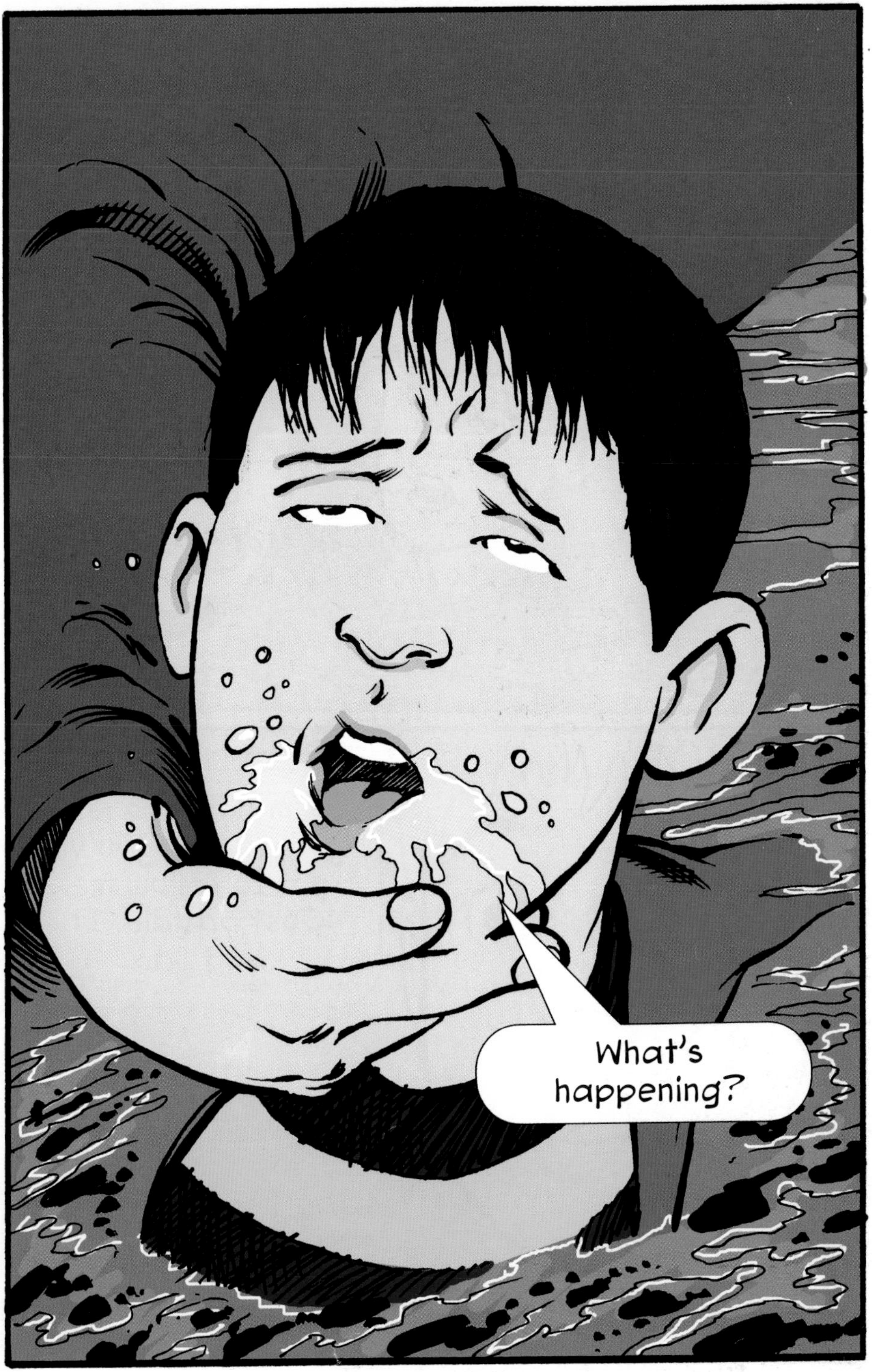
What's happening?

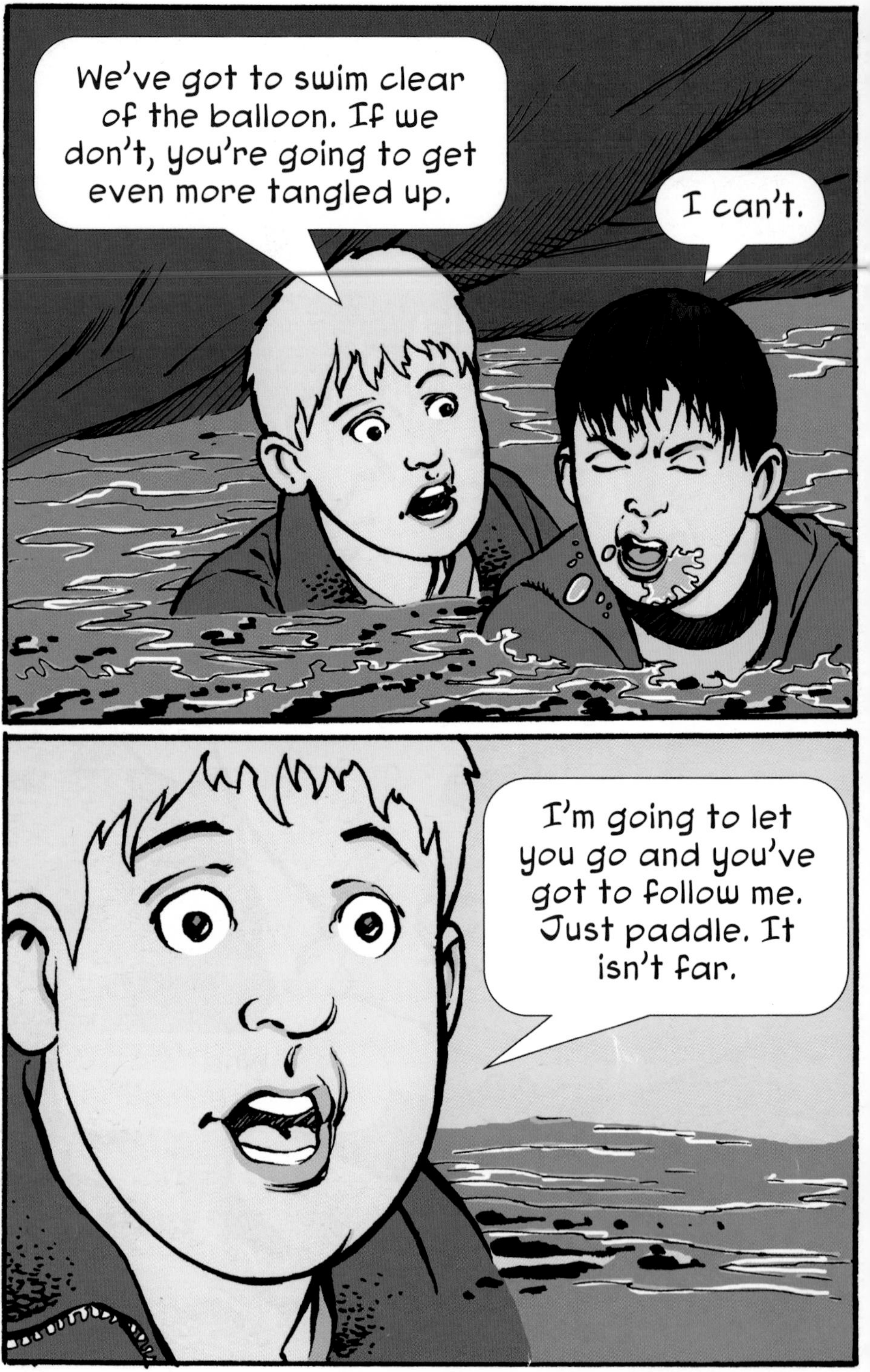
We've got to swim clear of the balloon. If we don't, you're going to get even more tangled up.
I can't.
I'm going to let you go and you've got to follow me. Just paddle. It isn't far.

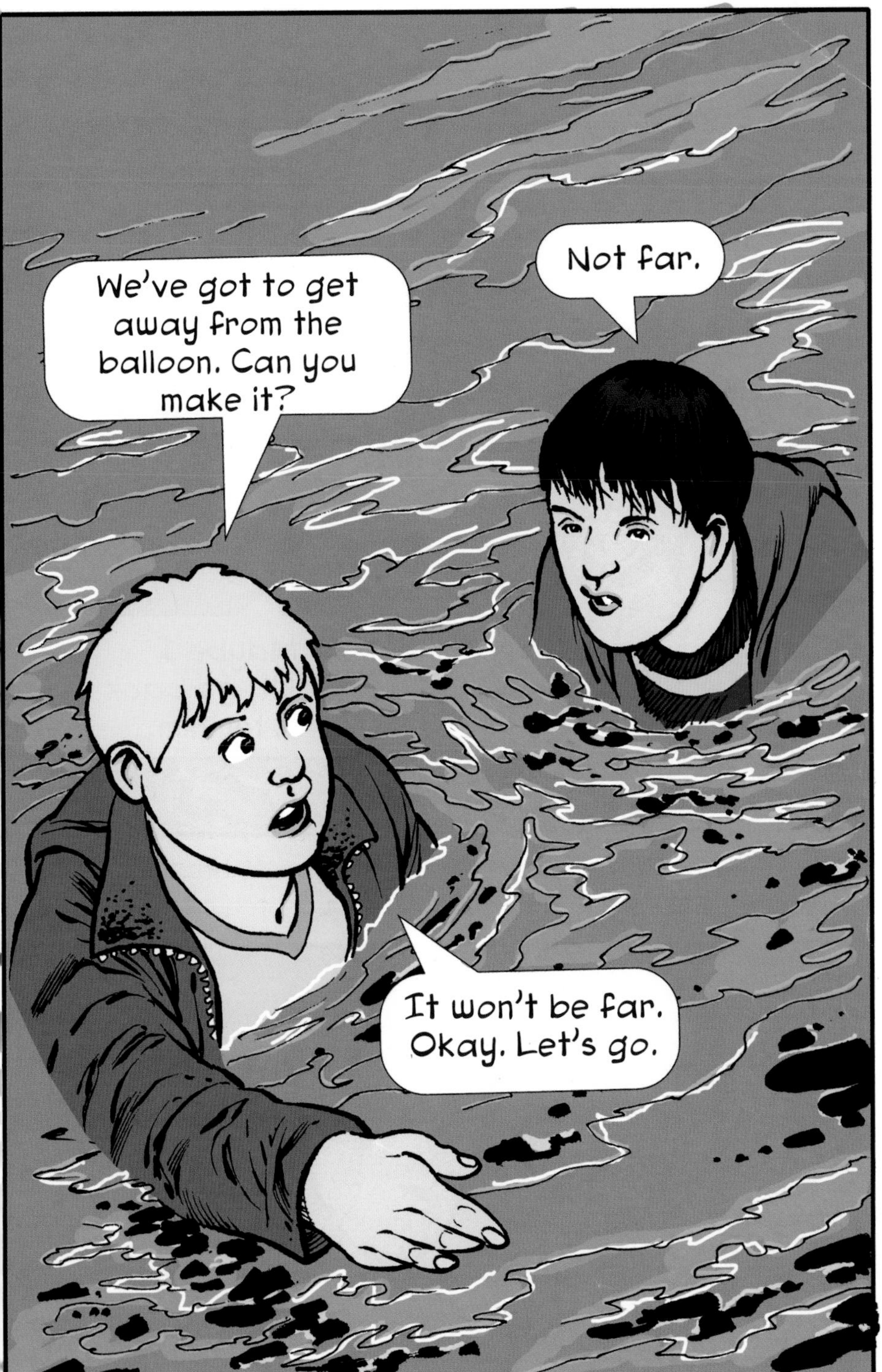
We've got to get away from the balloon. Can you make it?
Not far.
It won't be far. Okay. Let's go.

Chapter Seven

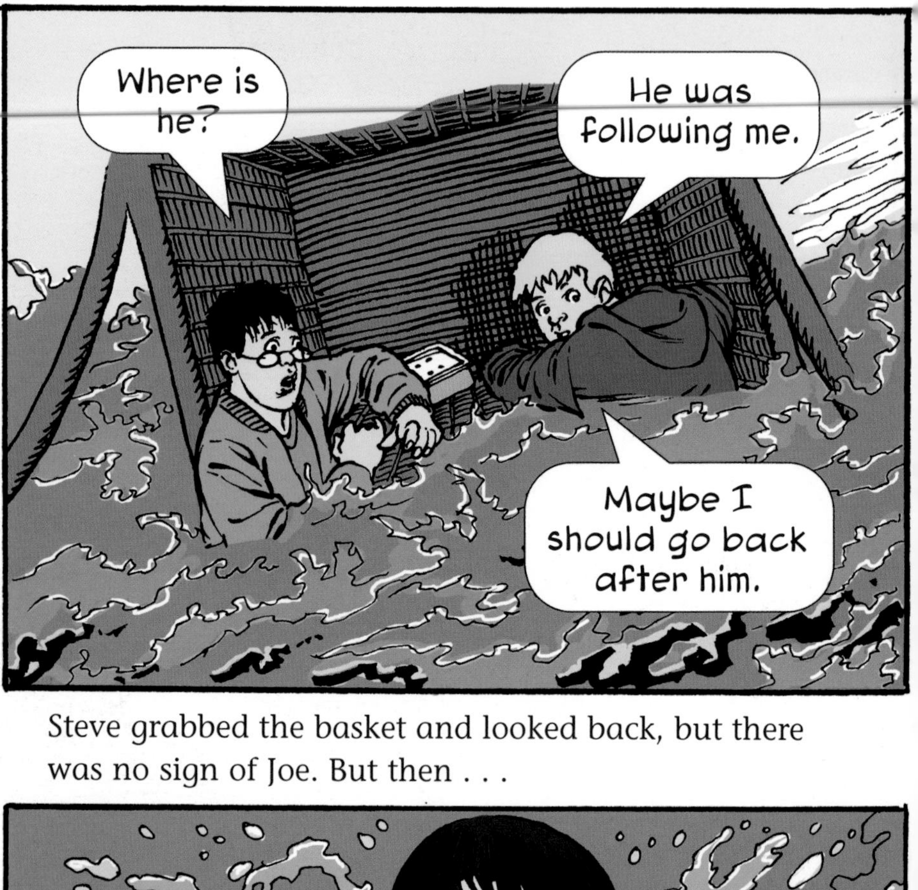
Where is he?
He was following me.
Maybe I should go back after him.

Steve grabbed the basket and looked back, but there was no sign of Joe. But then . . .

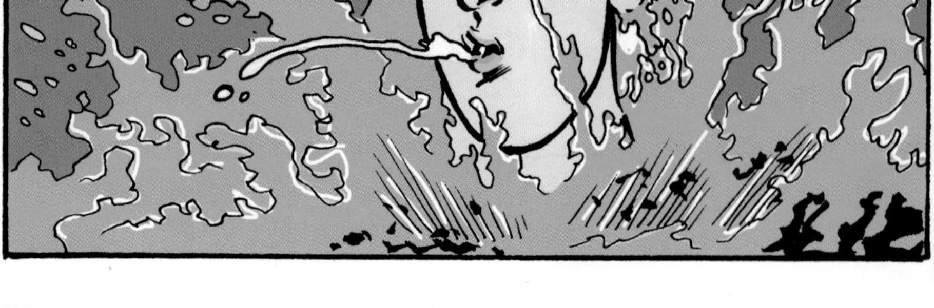

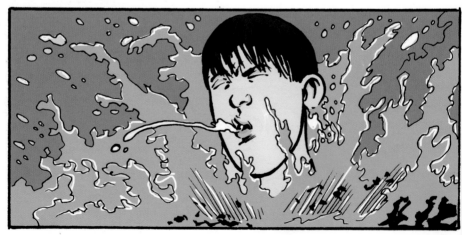

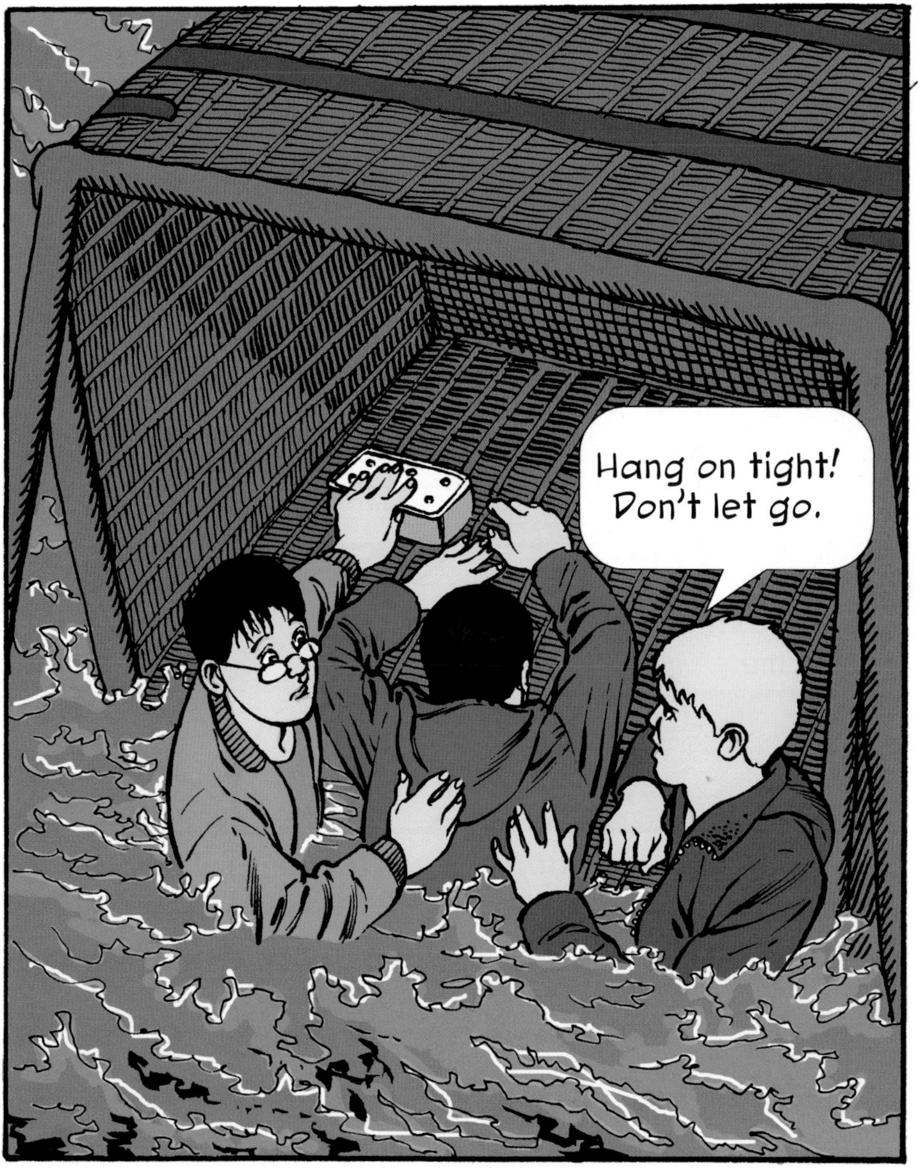
Hang on tight! Don't let go.

Steve had never felt so exhausted. All he wanted to do was give up, close his eyes, and slide down into the waves. The water felt strangely warm and inviting.

Then, just as Steve began to lose his grip on the basket, he heard an angry squeak.

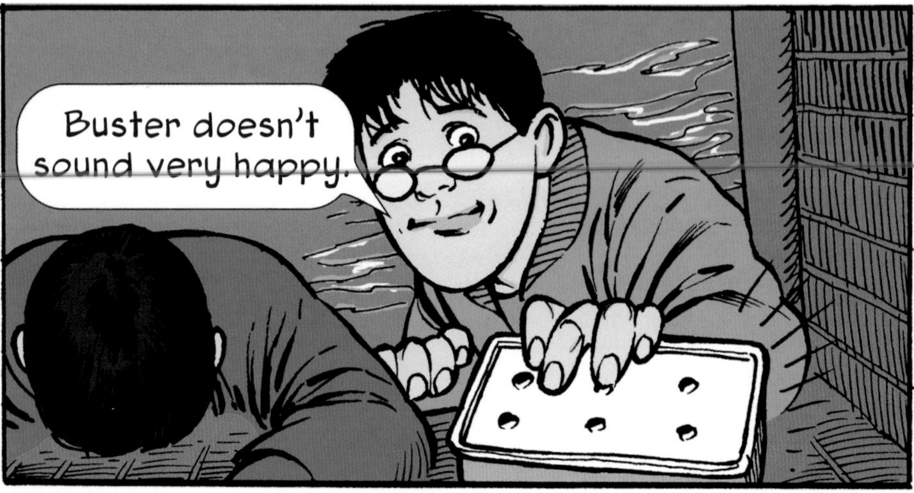
Buster doesn't sound very happy.

Steve felt a surge of energy.

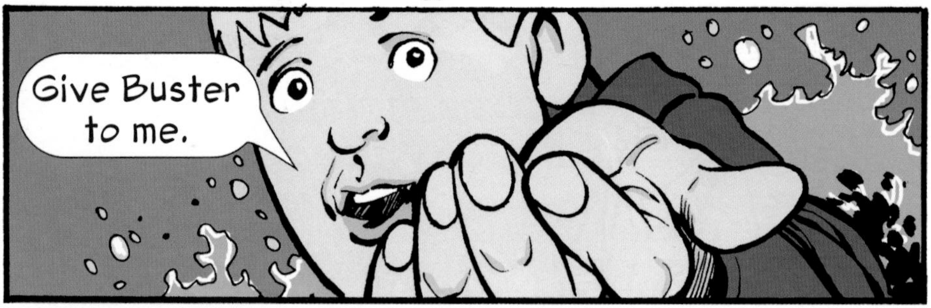
Give Buster to me.

Will's hand was shaking so much from the cold that the box slid out of his fingers.

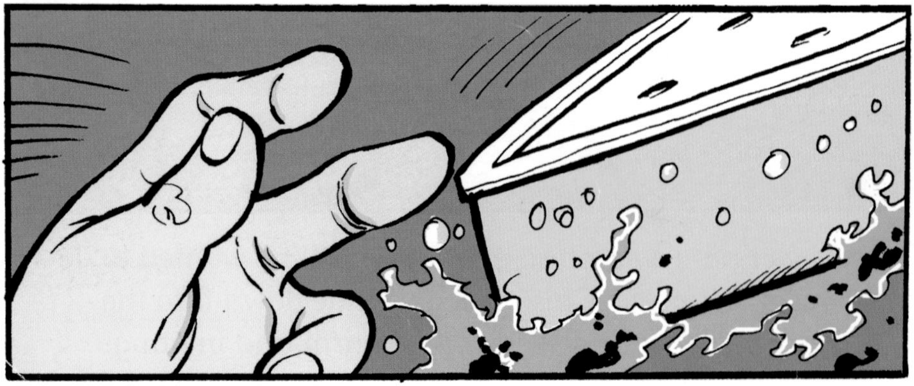

Steve launched himself after Buster in a fast crawl. He didn't feel tired now.

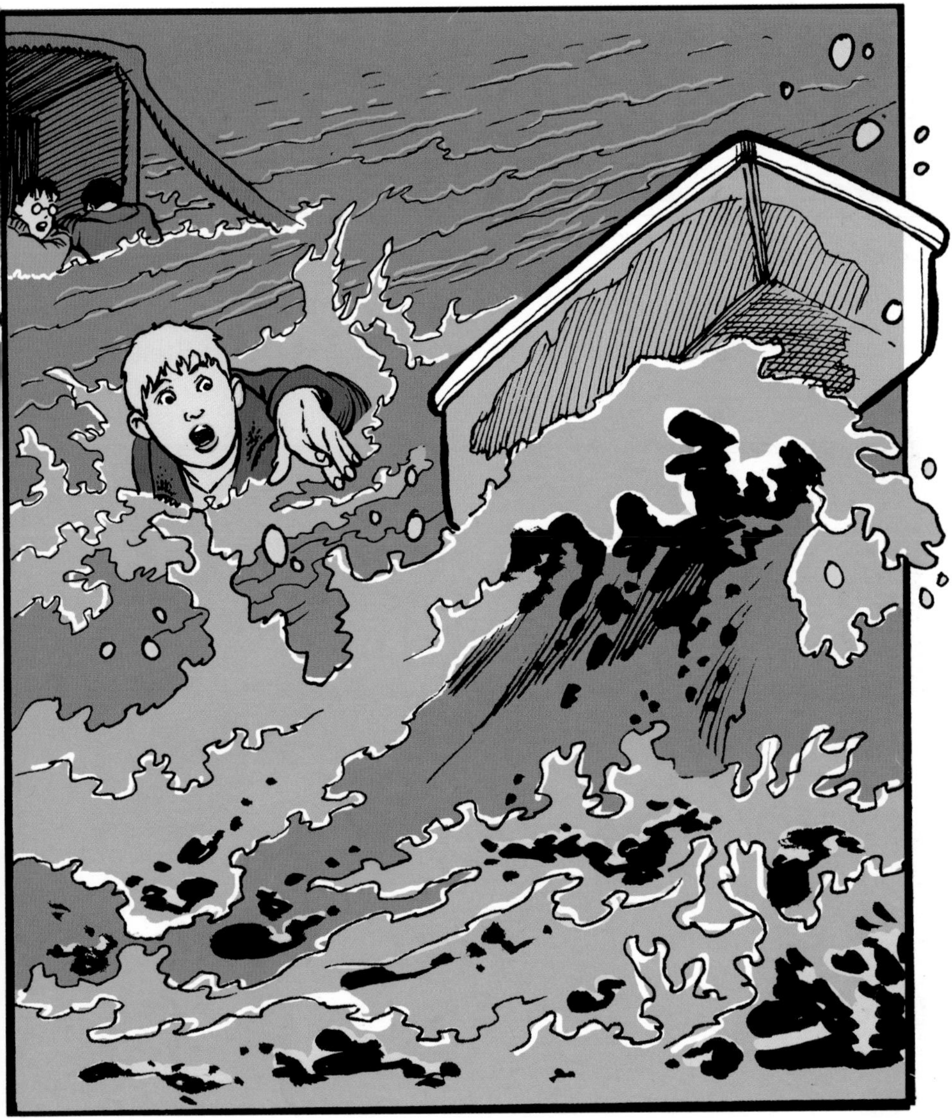

Out of the corner of his eye, Steve saw a lifeboat riding high on a wave.

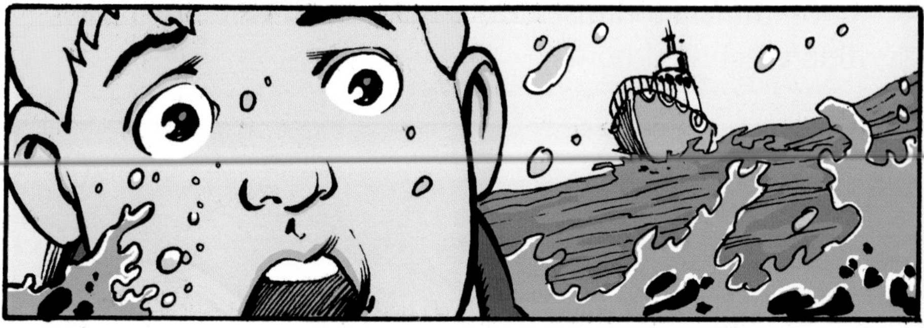

Someone was shouting at him now, but Steve didn't want to hear. All he could think about was rescuing Buster.

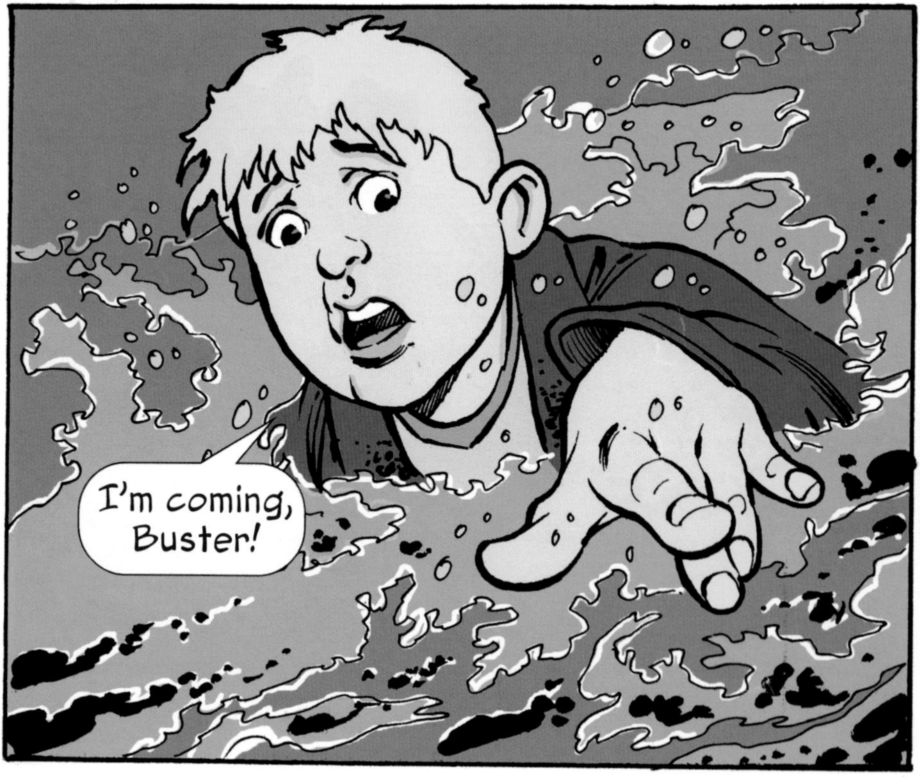
I'm coming, Buster!

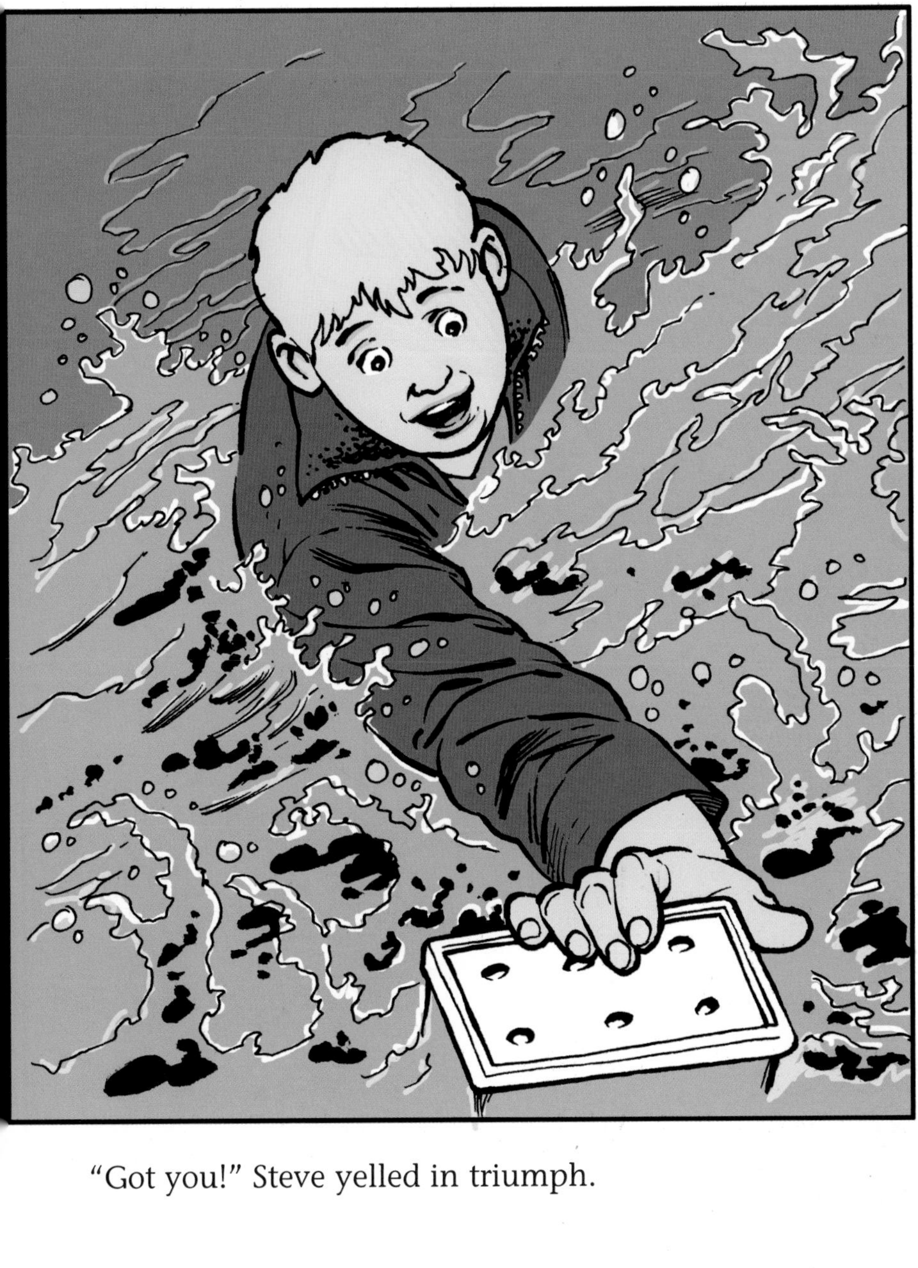

"Got you!" Steve yelled in triumph.

Steve couldn't keep going any longer. He was beginning to slow down.

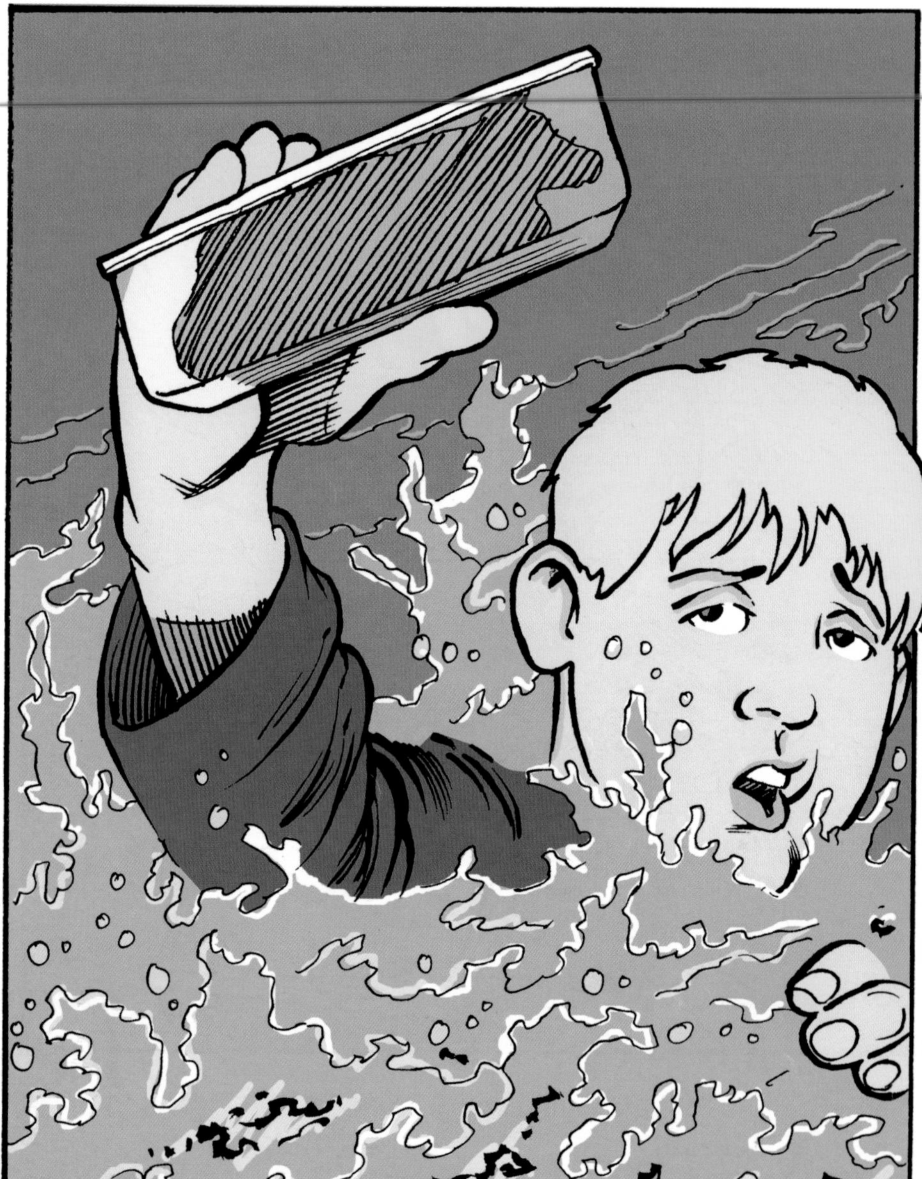

Someone grabbed the back of his jacket.

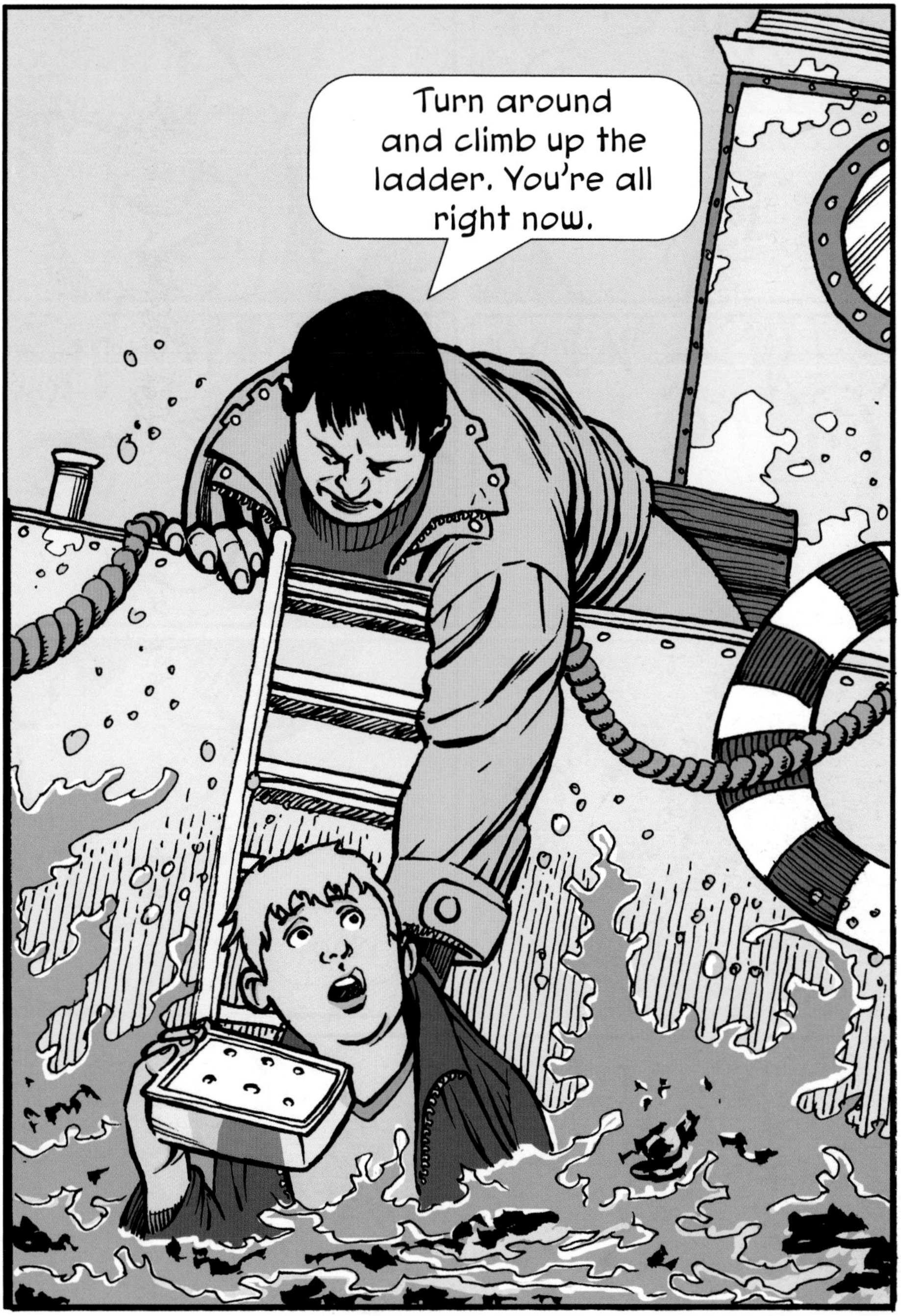
Turn around and climb up the ladder. You're all right now.

But Steve, still holding Buster's box in the air, was too weak.

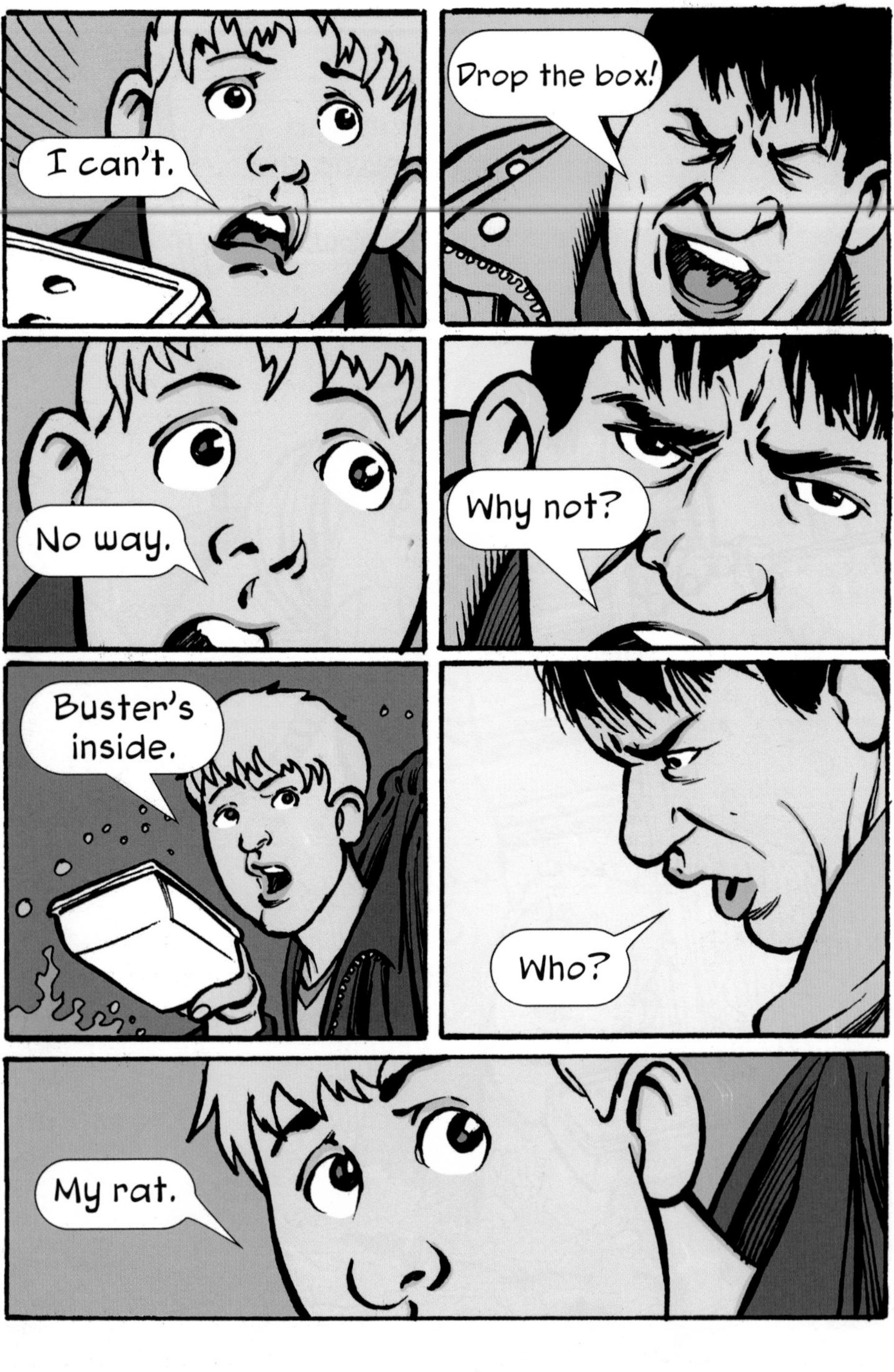

I can't.
Drop the box!
No way.
Why not?
Buster's inside.
Who?
My rat.

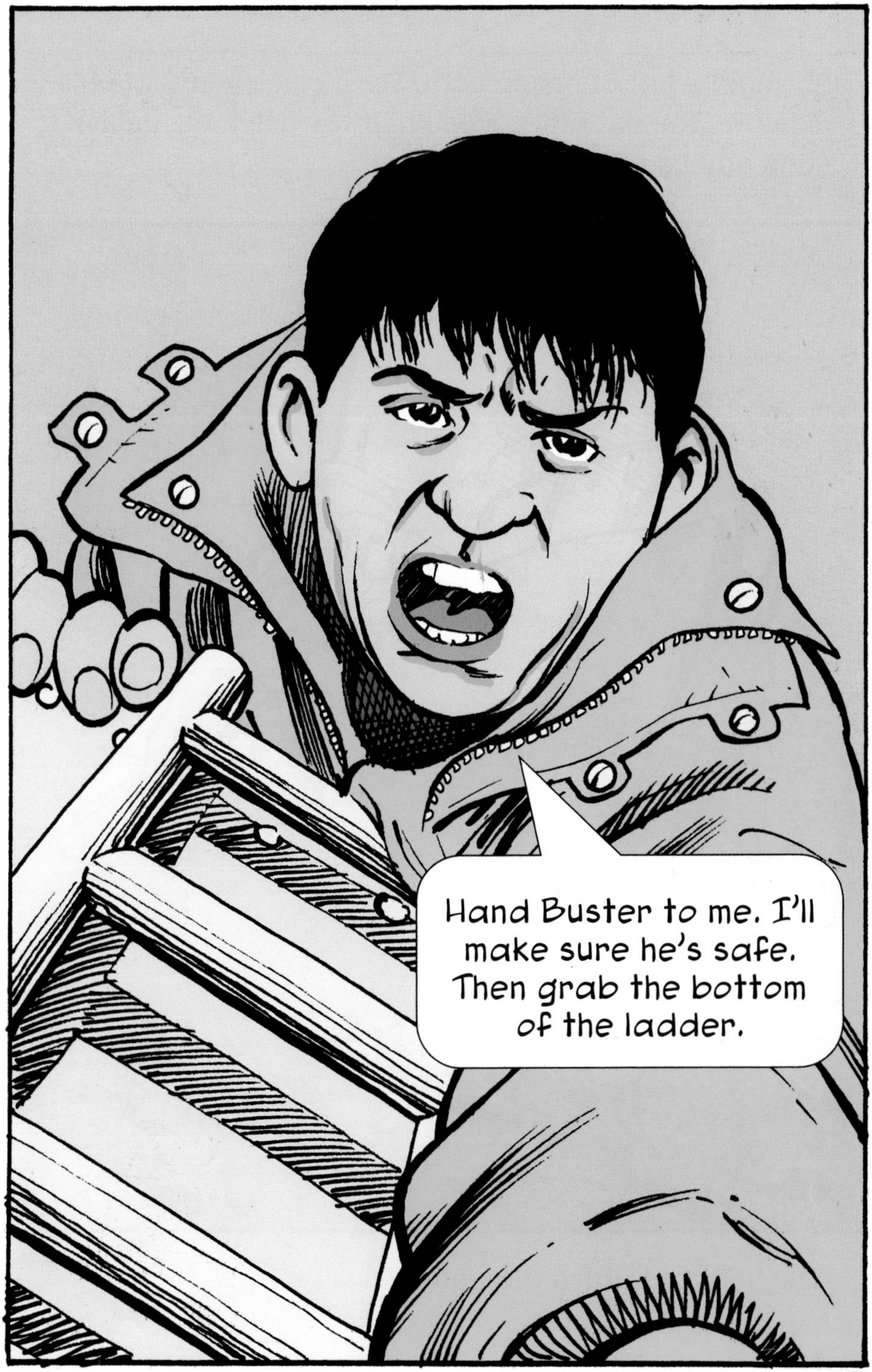
Hand Buster to me. I'll make sure he's safe. Then grab the bottom of the ladder.

Using the last of his strength, Steve passed Buster to his rescuer. The man then came halfway down the ladder and grabbed Steve.

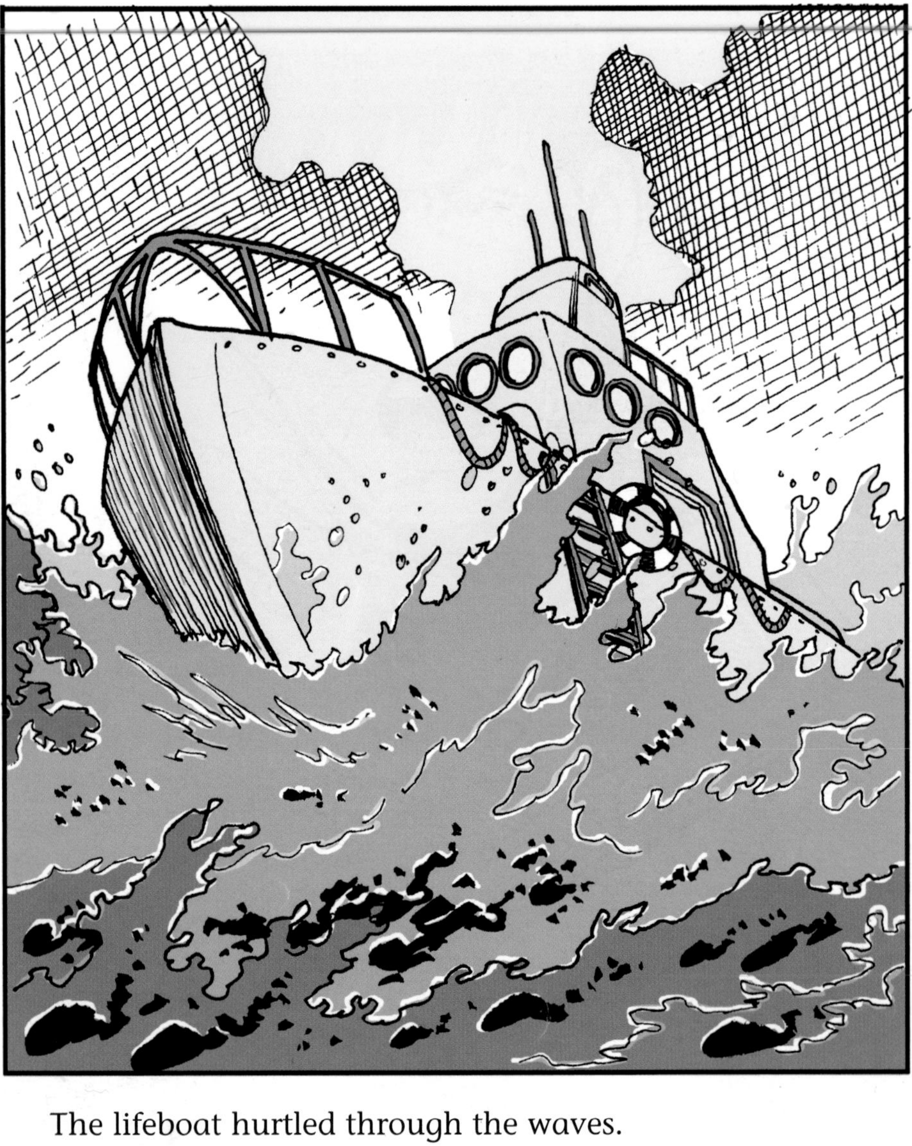

The lifeboat hurtled through the waves.

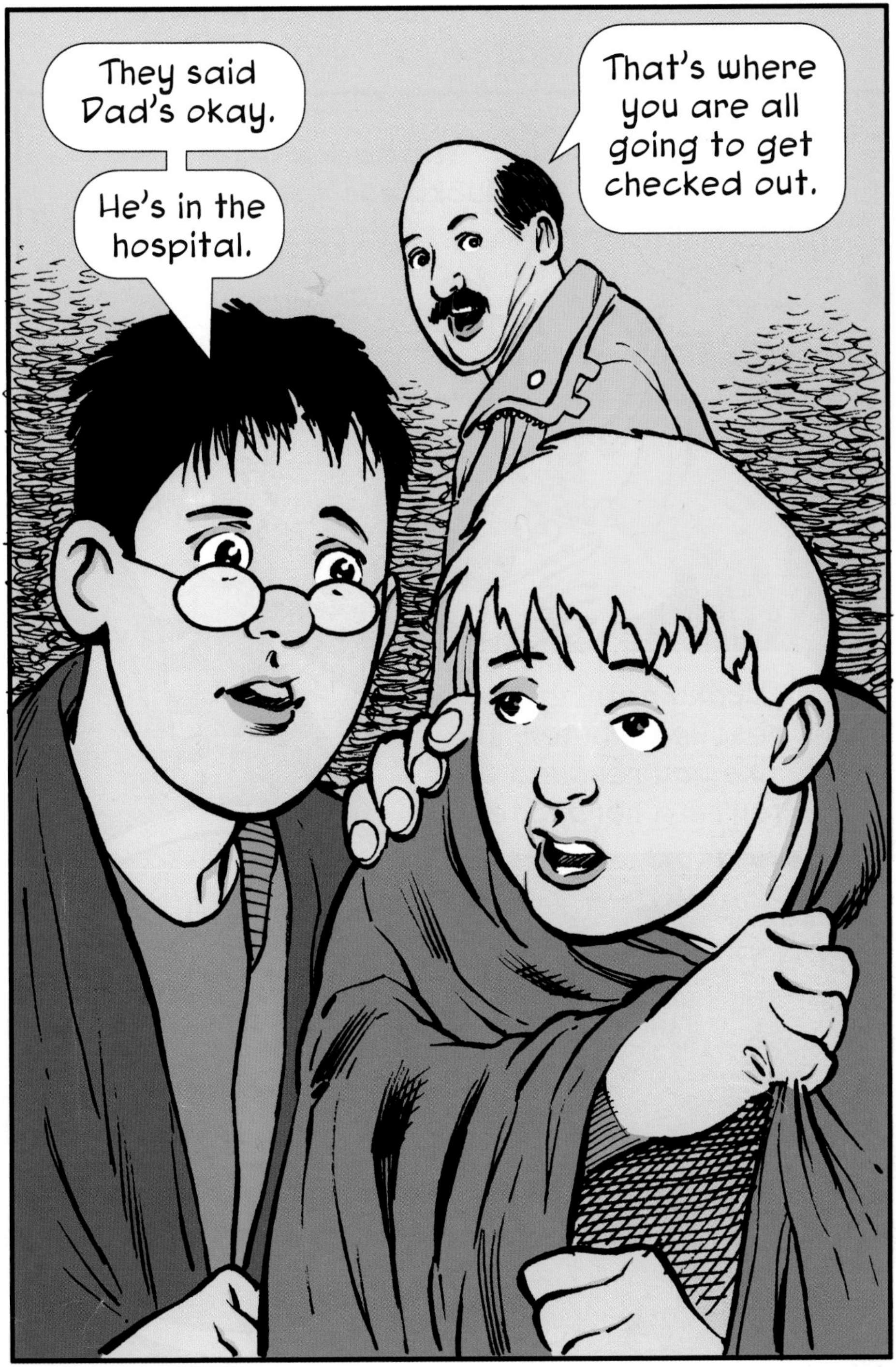
They said Dad's okay.
He's in the hospital.
That's where you are all going to get checked out.

Steve opened Buster's box to find that someone had given him a piece of cheese.

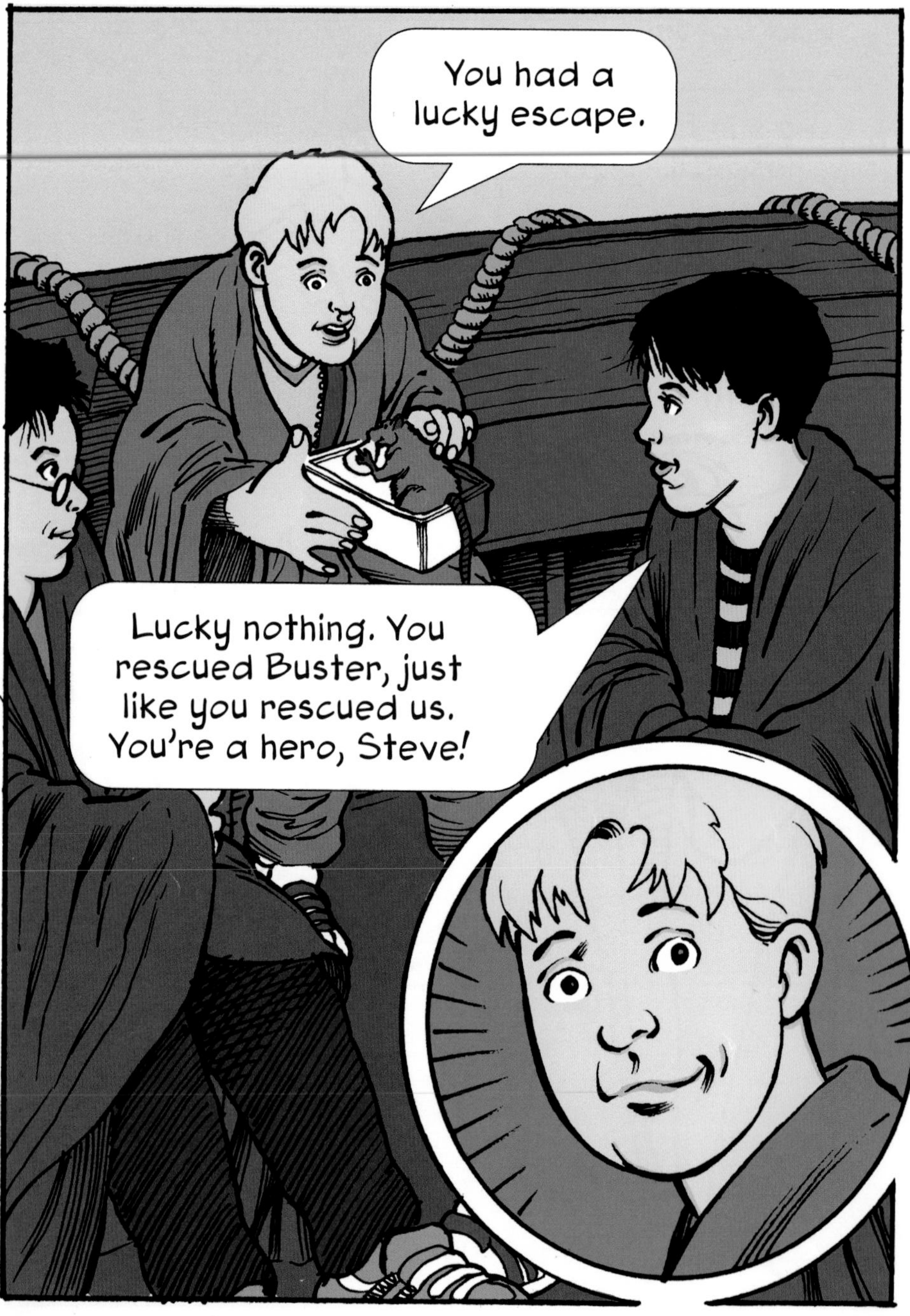
You had a lucky escape.
Lucky nothing. You rescued Buster, just like you rescued us. You're a hero, Steve!

ABOUT THE AUTHOR

Anthony Masters published his first book when he was 24. For the rest of his life, he wrote fiction and nonfiction for children and adults, winning awards along the way. *Junior Booklist* magazine once wrote that Masters knew how to "pack a story full of fast-moving incidents." Masters himself once said he would like to be a fox, because the creature is so cunning. Anthony Masters died in 2003.

GLOSSARY

churning (CHERN-ing)—moving roughly

mooring (MOR-ing)—fastening

muffled (MUFF-uhld)—softened

saturated (SATCH-uh-rate-id)—soaked completely

spray (SPRAY)—small drops of water that fly off the top of a wave

swell (SWELL)– a long wave or series of waves

toggle (TOG-uhl)—a small pin or rod that is used to hold things together, or can be used like a switch to operate machinery

INTERNET SITES

Do you want to know more about subjects related to this book? Or are you interested in learning about other topics? Then check out FactHound, a fun, easy way to find Internet sites.

Our investigative staff has already sniffed out great sites for you!

Here's how to use FactHound:

1. Visit *www.facthound.com*

2. Select your grade level.

3. To learn more about subjects related to this book, type in the book's ISBN number: **1598890867**.

4. Click the **Fetch It** button.

FactHound will fetch the best Internet sites for you.

DISCUSSION QUESTIONS

1. What do you think about this story? Is it believable? Why or why not?

2. How do you feel about the time and energy spent on saving Buster, the rat? Explain your thinking.

3. Do you think kids should be able to bring pets with them when they travel? Why or why not?

WRITING PROMPTS

1. Write about how and why the man rescuing Steve changed his attitude between pages 62 and 63.

2. Write and illustrate an adventure story of your own. Use a graphic novel format like this one.

3. If you had your own hot air balloon, where would you travel? Would you bring any friends along for the ride? Write about it.

ALSO BY ANTHONY MASTERS

JOKER
by Anthony Masters
WHO KIDNAPPED MAGIC MAX?
STONE ARCH Graphic Novel

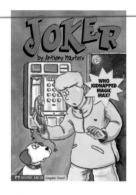

Joker

When Mel's dad, the magician, is kidnapped, no one believes him. Everyone thinks Mel is just joking. How can he convince them that he's telling the truth . . . and save his dad?

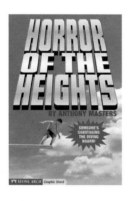

HORROR OF THE HEIGHTS
BY ANTHONY MASTERS
SOMEONE'S SABOTAGING THE DIVING BOARD!
STONE ARCH Graphic Novel

Horror of the Heights

Dean suffers from a fear of heights, which is a big deal when your brother's a diving champion. And someone is out to sabotage the diving board! He needs to expose that person . . . or his family is in danger.

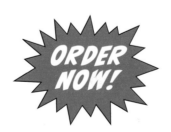